THE COUNTERATTACK

Books by Brien A. Roche

The Prohibition Series
The Last Stand
The Liberators
The Counterattack

Stuff We All Should Know
Law 101
Objections: Interrogatories, Depositions and Trial
Virginia Torts Case Finder
Virginia Domestic Relations Case Finder
Baseball Coaches' Handbook, Co-authored by Brien Roche

For more information
visit: www.SpeakingVolumes.us

THE COUNTERATTACK

Brien A. Roche

SPEAKING VOLUMES, LLC
NAPLES, FLORIDA
2024

The Counterattack

Copyright © 2024 by Brien A. Roche

All rights reserved. No part of this book may be reproduced or transmitted in any form or by any means without written permission.

ISBN 979-8-89022-151-3

To my 13 grandchildren

Acknowledgments

To my 13 grandchildren, none of whom have read this book, they did however inspire me.

Prologue

The Custer brothers were no strangers to conflict. Conflict hovered around them. Bos Custer had enlisted in the US Army in April 1917. He had not asked his two younger brothers to join him. They just did. No big surprise. They did everything together. On their father's pig farm in West Virginia, they wrestled pigs together, hunted together, fought together, and dealt with their father together.

Their father, Cookie Custer, had fled Alabama as a young slave and joined the US Army under then-Colonel George Armstrong Custer. Cookie's bravery and adaptability had won him the respect of Colonel Custer and his eventual freedom. He moved north with his recently freed wife and established a pig farm near Harpers Ferry, West Virginia. The business thrived, as did he and his wife. They had three sons who fought as storm troopers in Northern France for nearly 18 months. Their heroism and creativity were well-known to the troops. They returned home in early 1919 expecting a hero's welcome. They received nothing but bitterness and hatred.

On July 19, 1919, in the streets of Washington, DC, they fought back against a white mob interested in punishing the Black man for alleged transgressions that didn't exist.

They set up their own liquor distribution business coordinated with the pork distribution business they ran with their father. The alcohol distribution business was to generate profits to promote the Black community. The Custer brothers received a percentage on sales. It was enough to make it all worthwhile. At the time, there was no appreciation of the demand for alcohol. It was unlimited. The small margin of profit the Custers expected became huge as the operation increased in size. As profits soared, so did the antagonism from their white counterparts. Gun battles were frequent and costly.

Bos had vowed he would not back away. He now had a child and a beautiful wife. He had hoped he might be able to turn the business over to one or both of his brothers. They were both as competent as he, but the triad was the triad. A missing piece meant weakness or collapse. None of them could tolerate that.

They had done battle with Al Capone. He was not skillful, but he was persevering. That perseverance and willingness to shed the blood of others made him a worthy opponent. Now both groups of adversaries had to make a decision. Would it be a death struggle or was there some way for these competing businessmen to coexist?

Chapter One

Take 'em to the Tunnels
July 16, 1921
Hay Adams House

The brothers did not waste any time. They knew that Capone was on the run. Bos announced he would go in the front door. He directed Nevin and Thomas to look for side or back exits. What none of them knew was that Capone had explored the means of exit. He knew there was a basement tunnel that would take him to 17th Street where his car was parked.

Bos got to the third floor and moved to the south side of the house closest to the White House. All of the rooms were empty. Capone had left without packing. All of his belongings were where you would expect a man to leave them if he had no intention of leaving. He ran to the back side of the house and opened the window. He shouted to one of his brothers that Capone was not on the third floor. He directed them to cover the exits, saying he would search the second floor going down and try to flush him out. What he didn't know was there was no one to flush.

Capone had deserted his men and was leaving Washington, DC.

After 30 minutes of searching, Bos finally exited the back of the house. He sat down on the back stairway and hung his head. "How the devil did he get away?"

"He probably checked out the tunnels. Jack Sanders loved tunnels. Why can't other people?" said Thomas.

"You're right. He can use tunnels just like we did. Why not? After all this is America. Home of the free," Nevin said.

Bos stood up and shook his head. "Being Black ain't fun. You can't win. Either they take to the tunnels, or they put you in a tunnel. But no sense in complainin'. We need to get back to West Virginia. We've been away too long. It's Saturday. We should be in West Virginia by now."

"Watch out!" Nevin shouted.

A tall man with a .38 revolver stood in the doorway above Bos. He was one of Capone's men. Both Nevin and Thomas had their weapons slung over their backs and handguns holstered.

"I know I can't get all three of you, but there's only one of you that I want," the gunman said.

Before the man had finished his words, Bos dove to his left, unholstered the .45 on his right hip, and fired off two rounds. The man was pushed back by the impact and then fell forward down three stairs to the ground.

"Big brother, I'd say your flushin' technique was not very thorough. Should we go in and check for other stragglers?" Nevin asked.

"Nope. I'm gettin' out of here." Bos jumped to his feet and ran back toward the White House.

Together they ran back toward the truck that they had left parked on 17th Street.

Chapter Two

Capone on the Run
July 16, 1921
Washington, DC

"He's gone back to the place on 23rd Street. He liked that hotel," Nevin said.

"Let's just saunter down that way and see what we find," Bos said.

The three brothers walked toward their Model T. Bos got behind the wheel. Nevin cranked the engine.

"Head back to West Virginia," Bos said to his men waiting on 17th Street. "Here's $300 to pay for the gas and some entertainment." He handed one of the men three $100 bills.

"Man, I ain't never seen hundred-dollar bills," the man said.

"Keep your head down and stay out of trouble. You'll see a lot more of those. I'll meet you back in Harpers Ferry in a few hours. No alcohol. The cops will roust you if they smell any alcohol on your breath. Take care of the other guys," Bos said as he pulled away.

Bos went west on Pennsylvania Avenue for six blocks. He turned at Washington Circle and proceeded south on 23rd Street. The car he was looking for was in plain sight.

"Pull over in front of that four-door. That's it, isn't it?" Thomas said.

"Yep. Sure looks like it," Nevin said.

"You two get down in your seats. Let's wait and see if he comes out. My guess is he went into the hotel to get his things. Get your .45s ready. He's not goin' down quietly," Bos said.

Two hours of waiting didn't produce a thing. Bos saw the cigar in the distance. He knew it was Capone. He had one guy on each side of him. They walked two paces behind. Each was carrying a Thompson. No attempt to disguise.

"Wake up, sleepyheads. Here comes the man. Well protected. Well fed. They will head to 14th Street. Let's follow. Once we get them on the bridge, we'll see how they react to .45 slugs."

Fourteenth Street was only nine blocks east. Bos followed the Capone car. He kept his distance.

Once Capone was on the bridge, Bos told his brothers to roll down the windows.

"Nevin, here are three of my clips. Three for you, Thomas. Let's take out the guy ridin' shotgun first. Capone is in the back. He wouldn't know how to use a Thompson," Bos said.

Bos pulled up at a 45-degree angle behind and to the left of Capone. "Take a shot," Bos said to Thomas.

Thomas was good with a .45. One shot and the man in the front passenger seat slumped over.

Capone was lying on his side in the back of the car. The gunfire caused him to sit upright. He grabbed the Thompson from the front seat. He turned to his left and fired. The shots went high.

"Shoot out the tires," Bos said.

Nevin, from the backseat, shot out the right rear tire. The Capone car pulled to the right. The guardrail on the bridge was a wooden beam. It was no match for the heavy vehicle. The beam splintered. The car stopped at the edge of the bridge.

Bos pulled over next to the car. He unholstered his .45 and shot the driver three times in the chest. Now it was just Capone. Capone showed some athleticism. He had wiggled out the right-side window, stood on

The Counterattack

the edge of the bridge, and jumped feet first into the Potomac River. For a big man, he was graceful.

Traffic on the bridge had halted. Bos ran to the south side of the bridge. No sign of Capone. No sign of a floating body. Bos took off his right shoe and was removing the shoe on his left foot when Nevin approached.

"No. You're not jumpin' in the river," Nevin said.

"What's it look like?"

Nevin and Thomas both approached their brother. Together they restrained him. Nevin had him in an arm lock from behind. Thomas picked up his feet and put both feet in an arm lock. Together they carried him back to the car.

"This may hurt a bit. It's for your own good," Nevin said.

Nevin put his brother in a headlock, flexed his biceps, and applied pressure to both carotid arteries. Within 20 seconds, Bos had lost consciousness.

"Do you want the honors?" Nevin asked Thomas.

"You mean mouth-to-mouth?" Thomas asked.

"He'll come to on his own, but we may want to give him an assist."

"I'm here to help," Thomas said.

Once the air was pushed into Bos's airway, he began to stir.

"You poked the bear. You best be ready to deal with him," Thomas said.

"What the hell? Where is Capone?" Bos asked.

"He never surfaced. Must've drowned," Nevin said.

"What happened to me?" Bos asked.

"Blacked out. Damnedest thing I ever saw," Thomas said. "We had to catch you. Almost fell in the river."

"I agree. Darndest thing I ever saw too," Nevin affirmed.

Chapter Three

Back to Monica
July 21, 1921
Lady Monica Mine

Lady Monica was not acting like a lady.

Bos Custer had helped the miners out over a year ago. He wrote up a deal that both miners and management agreed to live with. Now someone had breached.

From the nearby mountaintop, Bos could see the women blocking the main entrance to the mine. He had been told that the women would not allow the men to go back into the mine. There were safety concerns. One of the deepest shafts was showing very high levels of methane. Another shaft had collapsed. The women were worried. They had reason to be. The owner had done little to maintain the mine. The miners were afraid to protest. This was their livelihood. This was all they knew.

The women had a different view. Their men wanted to work. The woman wanted them to work. But the women also wanted their men to come home at the end of the day.

A pickup truck with two men in the front and four in the back turned the corner. It drove up the slight incline to the main entrance to the mine. The large man in the passenger seat got out. Bos recognized him. Couldn't recall the last name. The first name was memorable. Ebeneezer. Not your ordinary name.

Bos couldn't hear the conversation. The body language was aggressive. Ebeneezer wanted the women to move away from the entrance. They refused. The four men in the back of the truck got out. Each was carrying an axe handle. They stood shoulder to shoulder with the axe handles in front of them. They began pushing the women away from the mine entrance. Some of the women laid down on the ground. Others locked arms and sat on the ground.

Ebeneezer was angry. He ordered the men to start dragging the women away. The women were kicking and screaming.

The women were all in their 20s. Most of them had three or more children. The leader of the crew was also the local schoolteacher. Martha was white. She was five feet nine and weighed 130 pounds. She had pulled up the leg of her dress. Her thin legs were muscled. The striations of muscle said this was a woman of some strength. She told two of the women to get behind one of the men with an axe handle. From behind, the two women pulled the man back while the schoolteacher grabbed his axe handle. She poked the man in the face. Blood streamed out of the man's nose.

Bos took aim with his Springfield. The shot was less than 200 yards. He shot out the right front tire of the small truck. Ebeneezer looked around. All of his men were still standing except the one with the broken nose. He looked at the truck and saw the right front tire. He dropped his hands.

"Custer, I know you're out there. We just want to open the mine. We're not looking to hurt anyone," Ebeneezer yelled.

Bos came down from his perch 200 yards away.

When he was 50 yards away, he said, "Our deal was you pay these men to work. They can't work if the mine is filled with gas. They can't work if the support beams collapse. What are you doin' to correct that?"

"We put large battery-operated fans to blow the gas out. We brought in larger beams to support the shafts. They're being installed later this week."

"I am glad to see you're being so reasonable. I knew you would." Bos stopped at the tree line. He shot out the front and back windows of the truck that Ebeneezer had come in.

"Just a reminder. I am keepin' an eye on things. The men get paid since the strike began. Get the work done pronto and get them back to work. I'll be watchin'. I also know where you live," Bos said. He turned and walked back to his perch. He would keep an eye on things.

Chapter Four

The Rats Are Coming
November 11, 1917
Paris, France

"There must be 100 of them," Nevin said.

"More than that. They're ridin' on top of each other," Bos said. The rats approached in the tunnel.

The French commander had asked for volunteers. The French were clever. A volunteer had the choice of 10 hours of hell and then double that number of hours of pleasure. Out of Bos's company of 160 men, all of them had volunteered for sewer duty. The first 30 were chosen. As the company's first sergeant, Bos picked the men. His brothers were automatic choices. The other 27 Bos chose on merit. Merit was in the eye of the beholder. The men knew the first sergeant didn't play favorites other than with his brothers. He was tougher on his brothers than he was on anyone else.

The theory was that the fighting had driven the rats toward Paris. Who knew? Maybe the rats just liked the Parisian food.

The job they were given was to clear out the sewers. Get rid of the rats. Sewer tunnels were interconnected with the stormwater tunnels. Bos had seen the same construction in DC. His father knew the tunnel network under Washington. He had bid on some of the tunnel construction jobs. He hadn't gotten the jobs because of the color of his skin. This was one time when the bias had cut in his favor. The jobs were dirty, filled with the unknown both as to outcome and payment.

Bos's father, Cookie Custer, liked the lesson he learned. Don't trust the federal government. Not all of their employees are out to promote the public good.

"Cover your ears," Bos said to his men in the tunnel.

Bos unholstered his .45 and fired a round above the rats. They stopped surging forward. It was like they thought in unison. The tide of rats slowed and turned around. Now they were moving away from the city. Bos followed them.

Another 30 yards, and he fired off another round. The surging herd of rats quickened their pace. The sound was deafening. Bos had looked at maps before entering the tunnels. This branch flowed toward the Seine.

"Brother, I hope these rats don't change their mind and do an about face," Nevin said.

"I'm more worried about all the rat shit. How do we ever get this smell out of our uniforms and boots?" Thomas said.

"I don't think we do," Nevin said.

"Napoleon was smart. He built the big avenues. He built the tunnels under the avenues. He thought that would help control the stench. He was wrong," Bos said.

"Hold your ears," Nevin shouted. Bos fired off another round. The light at the end of the tunnel was visible about 100 yards ahead.

What would happen when these hundreds of rats poured into the Seine? "You thinkin' what I'm thinkin'?" Bos asked his two brothers.

"I hope there is no one bathing in the river," Nevin joked.

"Even the French wouldn't do that," Thomas said.

"They may love us for our fightin'. I don't think they're gonna love us for herdin' the rats," Nevin said.

The Counterattack

The squealing sound increased. As the rats approached the waterway, they recognized their fate. A watery death was not in store. But a good dousing was.

Bos continued back through the tunnel. He explained to the men what was going on. He told them their presence had moved the rats along the tunnel to the river. The French would be appreciative. They always were. Good people to fight with. Good people to die with. Their rats were not so good.

"The good news is we've cleared one tunnel. Three more to go," Bos shouted out to the men.

His service in France was filled with contradictions. Appreciation from the French superiors. Acknowledgment from the French troops that they needed help to fight and defeat the Huns. Admiration from the French people for coming "over there" and shedding their blood.

But when shitty jobs had to be done, they always came to the Black troops.

Chapter Five

In the Holler
July 30, 1921
West Virginia

"We picked our land based on what the US Army taught us. Take the high ground," Nevin said.

"Why would you build your homes at the low end of the funnel? All of the mountains and hills around here funnel water. Water flows downhill. But people build their homes in the holler?" Thomas said.

"What they want is for us to help them move their homes or build new homes. These are simple people. Most of them have never seen a Black person before. It took some guts to come up here and ask for help. I say we help them. They may not be our friends. But they won't be our enemies," Bos said.

"I agree," Lee Ann said as she came into the room. "I'd also like to know why women are never consulted about these things." Rhonda was right behind her.

"I hope my husband is not in here making decisions for me without getting my input," Rhonda said.

"You know I wouldn't do that darlin'," Nevin said as he stood up. "We were just thinkin' out loud. Not makin' decisions."

"It's good to know you guys respect us. This operation don't work without us. Don't ever forget that. And don't take us for granted," Rhonda said.

The five of them were now standing in the dining room.

The Counterattack

"You heard what I said. I think we help these people. We can rebuild their little homes in a week or less. Put 'em on higher ground and who knows? Maybe they become our best customers," Bos said.

"I say we help. But we don't sell them our product. Pork is OK. Alcohol is not OK," Rhonda said.

Lee Ann smiled. "I like that."

"I'll tell him we'll start tomorrow. Twenty men. Over a week, we should be able to cut plenty of trees and build plenty of houses," Rhonda said.

Bos went into the front room with the other four.

"Mr. and Mrs. Jackson, we appreciate you comin' by. I've discussed this with the other family members. We can start tomorrow. Your men and women need to help us. Some of the homes we can move. Others will just have to be left there, and we will build new ones. Do you have any logs stockpiled?" Bos said.

"We have about 50 freshly cut oaks. They're sturdy. We piled them on the high ground. I say we build there," Jackson said.

"Tomorrow morning it is. We'll be there about 9:00 a.m. Could you send one of your people up to guide us to this place?" Bos asked.

Bos wondered how much these people had lost from the flooding. It couldn't be easy. These people had grown up here. Lived all their lives here. Married here. Died here. For them to pack up their belongings and their homes, meager as they were, was a whole lot.

Bos was strategic. These people may not be any immediate benefit. But long-term, these people could be of help. More than help. Maybe even friends.

Chapter Six

Where We Goin'
August 10, 1921
Harpers Ferry, West Virginia

Bos could hear the baby crying. He got up from the table and went upstairs. Ten minutes later, he returned with little George. The bottle of milk was cold. There was no refrigeration. Cooling consisted of using the cold water from the mountain stream. Even in the middle of summer it was no more than 55 degrees.

Bos resumed his seat next to his father.

"Did you program the baby cryin'?" Cookie asked.

"No. That was unplanned. But timely," Bos smiled.

"You bet. Now tell us what's in store for us. Unless of course you don't think we have a right to know," Cookie said.

"You have a right. I'm not askin' anything of you except from my wife. I would like your help, but I can do this without your help. My plan is to go straight at Capone. We said before 'no mercy.' He has more men than we can muster. He has more money than we'll ever have. So it's gonna be a guerrilla war. I'll be usin' my marksmanship skills to pick away at his operation. I figure in 30 days I'll have his guys so edgy they won't be willin' to work for him," Bos said.

"Pretty gutsy. Especially for a father and husband," Lee Ann said. "I am part of this operation. I do have some input. This venture may be a noble one, but it could also destroy this family. If any one of us is puttin' their neck on the line, then all of us do the same. We all know you are not a grandstander. You are a lone wolf. You need to put the lone wolf back in his cage. We hunt as a pack."

"I second that," Thomas said.

"I third it, if you can," Rhonda said.

Everyone looked back at Cookie. "I guess it's unanimous. Once it's done, then it's done. We get back to business," Cookie said.

"Okay. I can live with that. We'll work together. No one-man shows. We're not in competition with Capone. What he does in the Midwest and the Northeast is up to him. I just don't want him comin' into our region. The Mid-Atlantic and southeast is ours. We protect that area, and we go straight at him. All agreed?" Bos said.

"All agreed," they all chimed in.

"Thomas and I will make our first trip out to Chicago on Monday. Just reconnaissance. Information gatherin'. We already know where Capone lives. I'm not gonna touch his house. Not touch his family. But we will be touchin' him. That's priority one. Second priority is to gather information on where he is distributin'. I can't use Burke for that. He may want to help, but he can't. That is gonna take more effort on our part. All of us," Bos said.

Chapter Seven

Tulsa Tumult
August 11, 1921
Harpers Ferry, West Virginia

August in Harpers Ferry could be beautiful. From the back porch, they could see the sun setting. The baby had been put down for the night.

"Can you see him kickin'?" Lee Ann said.

"Kickin' like a mule," Bos said.

"You look like you've been thinkin'. Always dangerous?"

"Haven't you heard about Tulsa?" Bos asked.

"No. What happened in Tulsa?" Lee Ann said.

"They tried to call it a riot. Wasn't no riot. Just a massacre. A plain old massacre. They said some 19-year-old Black kid assaulted a white woman. He tripped while he was in an elevator and touched the arm of the white elevator operator. Rumors spread that she had been raped. Wasn't no rape. The Black part of North Tulsa was burned to the ground. Over 1,000 homes destroyed. Three hundred people killed. Nine thousand left homeless. What a waste."

"That couldn't happen on the East Coast."

"What do you think almost happened in DC two years ago? If we hadn't fought back, they would've burned LeDroit Park. You know that as well as I."

"You're right," she paused. "How come I haven't been readin' about this in the papers?"

"I don't know. I suspect it has to do with who owns the papers. I'm gettin' my news from our little wireless machine in the living room. It carries the baseball games and the news. As far as I know, they're both reported correctly."

"I hope you're not lookin' for a new cause."

"No new causes. Just a renewed commitment. We need to create wealth. We need to do it through the Black churches that have joined with me. With wealth comes power. With power we have the ability to do good. That's what I want to do."

"You are a dreamer. That's for sure. But that's also why I love you."

"Don't get no better than that."

He reached out for her hand. "Let's take a walk."

Chapter Eight

Recon
August 25, 1921
Southside Chicago

The three brothers felt like they were back in northern France. Their success as storm troopers rested on their reconnaissance. Seldom did they rely on information about the enemy that they had not gathered themselves. Information was gold. They did their own mining. They used the same tactic with the South Side Gang. Bos, Nevin, and Thomas gathered their own information.

They knew that Torrio's outfit had brokered a peace with the northside outfit run by Dean O'Banion. The O'Banion crime family was of mixed ethnicity. Torrio's crime family was all Italian.

O'Banion didn't trust Torrio. Torrio didn't trust O'Banion. The Custers tested the limits of that mistrust.

O'Banion's home on the north side of the city was modest. Thomas and Nevin had been surveying the house for two days. They dressed as sanitation workers. Sweeping the street only took so long. Together they swept both sides of the street for a block on either side of O'Banion's home. Then they set up a barricade around a manhole that was two doors down from O'Banion's house. They spent the rest of that first day in and out of the manhole.

What they learned was that O'Banion left the house at 6:00 a.m. He returned at 6:00 p.m. He spent most of his day at a flower shop. Schofield's Flower Shop was near the corner of West Chicago Avenue and North State Street. O'Banion extorted the owner of the flower shop. He acquired a half interest in the shop. O'Banion was fond of flowers.

The Counterattack

He was an excellent arranger. He became the flower arranger for all mob funerals in Chicago. Business was brisk.

At 10:00 p.m. on August 25, 1921, Bos Custer, acting alone, broke the front display window of Schofield's Flower Shop. He entered the business through the broken window. With an axe handle, he broke many of the flower vases and destroyed the flowers. The business was a mess. It took Bos two minutes to wreak havoc. Then he departed.

Neighbors had seen a masked man break the window, enter the shop, and then exit. He left the flower shop area riding a motorcycle. Two other motorcyclists joined him at the nearby intersection.

The police called O'Banion at 11 o'clock that night.

"Who the hell would do this?" O'Banion asked the beat cop. "Don't they know who I am? I could crush them."

"It sure looks like this was an attempt to send a message to you, Mr. O'Banion," the beat cop said.

"Not everything is about messages," O'Banion said.

By midnight, O'Banion's two lieutenants had arrived at the flower shop. "This was not random," O'Banion said. "This had to come from Torrio. But why? Our deal is working. We're all making money."

Shortly after midnight, one of O'Banion's runners came in. Out of breath. He blurted out, "The warehouse is on fire."

"What the devil are you talking about?" O'Banion asked.

"The warehouse. The liquor. It's all on fire," the runner said.

"Maybe the copper was right. It is a message. I need to find out who the messenger is." He looked at his two lieutenants. "Call Torrio. We need to talk now."

Within 10 minutes, Johnny Torrio was on the phone. "I'm suspicious, Johnny. First a break-in. Now a fire. This has got to be somebody from your outfit," O'Banion said to Torrio.

"No. It makes no sense, Dean. We just made a deal. A good deal. Why would I break it?"

"I don't know. But I didn't destroy my flower shop. I didn't burn my warehouse. The two happening in one night is not a coincidence," O'Banion said.

Bos, Thomas, and Nevin arrived back at their hotel by 1:30 a.m.

"Good night's work, brothers. Tomorrow, we give Torrio a lesson in tire slashin'. I figure we can cut at least 50 tires by 8:00 a.m. He'll think O'Banion did it. By the close of business tomorrow, they should be at war." Bos smiled.

"You do know how to ruin a guy's summer," Thomas said.

"Oh no. It's gonna be more than just a summer. It's gonna be a whole enterprise." Bos said.

"I was talkin' about my summer," Thomas smiled.

Chapter Nine

Turncoat
August 26, 1921
Chicago, Illinois

At 6:00 a.m., he knocked on the door. It only took one rap. The Custer brothers were on their feet with guns drawn. Nevin stood by the door hinges. Bos was on the other side. Thomas was low by the window with his .45 pointed at the door.

"Who is it?" Nevin said.

"I'm one of O'Banion's guys. I know who you are. I know why you're here. I can help," the voice said.

"Who's with you?" Bos said.

"I'm alone. No one knows I'm here."

Bos decided to open the door. Through the crack in the opening, he could see one man. The overhead light in the hallway did not cast any shadows, suggesting the man was alone. Bos opened the door the rest of the way, pointing his .45 at the man. Bos ordered the man to step back.

He stuck his head further out the door. He saw no one. Bos beckoned to the man to enter.

Once inside, Bos told him to lean up against the wall. His brothers kept their muzzles pointed at the man while Bos did a quick frisk.

"I got a .38 on my left hip," the man said.

"Can't leave home without it," Bos said.

"I've got a knife on my left calf," the man said.

Bos removed both weapons. He looked at the knife. The 12-inch blade was impressive. "Bear huntin'?" Bos asked.

"The boys joke it's for another type of hunting."

"State your business and be quick," Thomas said.

"O'Banion and Torrio both know that you're behind the flower shop rampage. They're both looking for a way to make peace. I'm here to tell you what they are up to. I'll do it for a fee. Once I finish, I'm out of here," the man said.

"Why should we trust you?" Thomas replied.

"You shouldn't," the man said. "Check me out."

"Why should we bother? You want to leave here alive; you tell us what you know," Bos said. He hit the man with the back of his hand. The man fell back and grabbed the wall as if there was something to latch on to.

"Okay. I get the message. If you don't kill me, O'Banion will. I'm a dead man either way. I make some money from you and move on, or O'Banion comes for me. I'm sick of his double-dealing. We do all the dirty work, and he gets all the rewards."

"Give him $300," Bos said to Nevin. "Let's hear what you got to say."

The money changed hands.

"You pack quite a wallop," the man said. He stroked the right side of his face. Bos did not wear any ring on his right hand. The man's right cheek was bleeding. Bos's large knuckles impacted the man's cheek bone, causing an abrasion and bleeding. He wiped the blood on the back of his pants.

"O'Banion plans to double-cross Torrio and Capone. Tomorrow night, eight men are going to Torrio's home. The plan is to kill him. At the same time, eight men will go to Capone's home to kill him. With the two of them out of the way, the northside gang of O'Banion controls Chicago," the man said.

"The agreement they reached doesn't count?"

"Nope. O'Banion figures Capone will only honor it so long as it suits him."

"I like that. We need to beat him to the punch. What else?"

"That's it. Ain't that enough?"

"I guess. Now take your money and get out of here."

Chapter Ten

Preemption
August 26, 1921
Chicago, Illinois

"This is only going to work if we operate as one-man teams. We know that Torrio has as many as eight men guarding his house. The same is true with Capone. We strike tonight. I'll take Capone's house. Remember the garrote? The French taught us how to use it. It's simple, quiet, and deadly. Thomas, you take Torrio's," Bos said.

"So one man is supposed to kill eight?" Nevin asked.

"We can do it. It's all about surprise. We know Torrio's guys are lazy. They like to sleep on their post. They got a few strong points. A few veterans. We know where they are. We know how they operate," Bos said.

Bos walked over toward his sea bag. He reached inside. He pulled out a long string that had two small pieces of wood attached to it. The garrote had originated during the Spanish Inquisition. It was an instrument of torture. Over the centuries, it had taken on different forms. The one that Bos and his brothers had used in Northern France was a simple piece of string with two wooden hand holds—one to push the noose closer around the neck and the other to pull it tighter.

The French had taught them that it took five minutes of pressure to kill a man. Bos had found it could be done much quicker. He threw one of the garrotes at Thomas, the other at Nevin. The third he kept and worked the action to make sure it worked as he had remembered.

The problem with the garrote in Northern France was getting the noose over the German helmet. Plus many German soldiers wore a strip of leather around their neck as protection against knives. Once the garrote slipped over the helmet, the leather stripping was no defense. Between the three Custer brothers, they had used their garrotes hundreds of times.

"Nevin, you'll drive. We know what their routine is. The spokes of a wheel. They have four guys going out from the house and four guys that surround the house. We take out the spokes. Then we move toward the hub."

Chapter Eleven

The Treaty
August 26, 1921

Bos had heard about it. He had often thought of what the war was all about. Nobody could tell him. He knew the US had not signed the Versailles treaty. The other European nations had. The US Senate refused to approve it. The treaty that brought the war with Germany to an end was signed August 25, 1921, between the US government and the Weimar Republic, the tail end of the Second Reich. Bos had been following the news on radio. He didn't really know what it all meant. To him and his brothers, it was just more confusion. Why wait two years to end a war? Why not sign the same treaty that the other allies had signed? Why not join the League of Nations that Wilson had proposed? Why not agree to Wilson's Fourteen Points?

None of it made sense. Bos loved to read. He started the novel by John Dos Passos. *Three Soldiers* had confused Bos. For the 18 months he had been in Northern France, he thought very little of why he was there. He had volunteered. His brothers had volunteered. His father before him had volunteered and fought in a different type of war. His father's war had accomplished something. It ended slavery. It restored the Union.

Bos knew that his war had meaning. He just couldn't find it. Dos Passos didn't help him. It was like the war had no meaning. He knew it did. He and his brothers hadn't killed hundreds of men for no reason. There had to be a reason. There had to be a reason for everything. His job was to find it.

The Counterattack

There had to be a reason why he had gone to war with Capone. He knew what that was. He was going to use the leadership skills he had learned in the US Army. Put them to good use and help his family. Just as Cookie had used his leadership skills to build a business. To raise a family. To teach his sons how to be men. Bos Custer would do the same.

His mother had taught him well. Everything he needed to know was in two books. Neither was written by Dos Passos. One of the books was the *Iliad*. It taught Pietà. It wasn't piety. It was duty, honor, and loyalty. The other book was the *Odyssey*. Happiness is at home. That's all he knew. That's all he wanted to know. He didn't care what Dos Passos said about the war. He knew what the war was all about. Pietà and coming home. He had both.

Chapter Twelve

Sticky Bombs
August 26, 1921
Chicago, Illinois

"No question they're quick on their feet," Nevin said. "We used the garrote on six of Torrio's men. No survivors. But still no Torrio. There's a reason they call him the Fox."

"If we can't find the prey, we'll find what they prey with. Remember the sticky bombs? We destroyed a whole fleet of German airplanes. The Germans never knew what hit 'em. When they saw the wreckage, they thought it was artillery. It was just the Custer brothers," Nevin laughed.

The Germans thought they had carefully hidden over 20 biplanes in Northern France. Their pilots were getting a well-deserved rest when the Custer brothers happened upon them. Twenty grenades with pins pulled and stuck to the wings in cowpies became easy targets for the sharp shooting Custer brothers. As each cowpie was hit, the grenade armature sprung open, destroying the plane.

"We don't have the cow pies, but we do have plenty of glue. Torrio has 50 trucks parked at his warehouse. They're all loaded with booze. Two grenades on each truck, front and back, ought to create a nice firestorm," Bos said.

"I agree. A little glue on the armature after the pin is pulled and a little glue on the side of the grenade to stick it to the truck should work. We can set up about 50 yards away. Three Springfields in the hands of the Custer boys should have all of those trucks on fire in less than five minutes," Thomas said.

The Counterattack

"The night is still young. I'd say we get movin'," Bos smiled.

The warehouse was less than a mile from Torrio's home. It was in the Levee District of South Chicago. The three-acre lot was surrounded by eight-foot-tall chain-link fencing. Three German shepherd dogs patrolled inside the fencing. The one security guard was armed with a shotgun and a .38 handgun.

The dogs were a challenge. Nevin had the idea of cutting open six steaks and lacing them with pepper. They threw the six steaks over the fence. The dogs ripped open the meat. The dogs were crying. Tears running out of their eyes. It was scary to see huge dogs that had lost control. They couldn't stop shaking their heads and sneezing. Nevin and Thomas climbed over the fence with large burlap nets. Each dog was quickly subdued and tied up in the net.

The security guard heard the ruckus. He came running, shotgun ready. Bos tripped him as he came around the back end of one of the trucks. He took the shotgun away from him and tied him to a nearby light post. So there was no doubt as to who the intruders were, Bos put a garrote around the man's neck and nailed the loose end to the wooden light pole above the guard's head.

"Probably not a good idea to try to get away. These garrotes are quite effective," Bos said to the guard.

The sticky bombs were a challenge. Some of the grenade armatures didn't want to stay closed. The few premature explosions caused no physical injury to the Custers. One grenade was put on the front hood of each truck. One grenade was placed inside the rear of the tailgate of each truck. The front grenade would destroy the engine. The back grenade would set the alcohol on fire.

Torrio's organizational obsession was apparent. The trucks were in three columns of 16 each. Exiting the fenced area was no more difficult than entering. The dogs were still tied up in the burlap nets. Their nostrils had calmed down. The barking continued. One of the dogs had succeeded in biting through the burlap. Nevin was the last to exit the fenced area. As he reached the top of the fence, the dog jumped for his foot. The leather combat boots that he wore protected him. He pulled the dog three feet off the ground with the dog clinging to his right boot. The dog would not let go. Nevin had some more ground pepper in his pocket. He reached in and pulled out a handful and threw it at the dog. The dog dropped to the ground.

"Nevin, you take the column farthest from the entrance. Thomas, you take the middle column, and I'll take the last column. Thomas's shots are the most difficult. We can help him out," Bos said.

They set up in different positions 50 yards from the fenced compound. Hitting a 5-inch grenade from 50 yards was something the Custer brothers were used to. They could hit a squirrel from 100 yards with a .22 rifle. The picking was easy. The resulting fire was glorious.

"You didn't need our help after all," Nevin said to Thomas.

"I was wonderin' what took you two so long," Thomas replied.

"I think a few of my shots ricocheted over to your trucks. That's the only reason you finished with us," Bos said.

Chapter Thirteen

7244
August 27, 1921
Chicago, Illinois

The single-family home at 7244 S. Prairie Avenue was two stories. Capone had begun living there two months earlier. The public records showed the house was titled in someone else's name. Capone's wife, Mae, and their son lived in a different location.

Bos knew the guards walked north on South Prairie up to 71st Street, turned left and then came down to S. Indiana Avenue, took a left on 74th over to South Calumet, and turned left going up to 71st. Sometimes they would change the route. They were never gone more than 15 minutes. The other guard walked in the opposite direction. Their meeting point was always 72nd and South Prairie. Bos knew the pattern. There were only two on patrol. That meant there were two more in the house. The others were asleep.

There was an alley between South Prairie and South Calumet on 72nd Street. Bos waited in the alley. He could hear the man shuffling toward him. No doubt tired. He'd been on his feet for several hours. His butt was heavy. His feet were dragging. Bos sensed he was easy prey. He walked out of the alley behind the man. Capone's men wore hats. This one did not. All the more accommodating for the garrote. Bos stepped up behind him, slipped the noose over his head, thrust forward with his left hand on the wooden handle, and pulled back with his right hand. There was a gurgle sound that came from the man's mouth. He reached back toward his throat with both hands. Bos tightened the noose. He pulled the man back into the alley and then drove his right shoulder into the back of the man's head. He heard the snap. The body went limp.

Bos left the body by the townhouse on that side of the alley. He knew the other guard had arrived at 72nd and South Prairie. His instructions were to not wait more than 60 seconds. If the second guard didn't show up, he was to return to the Capone house and prepare for the attack.

Bos approached the figure waiting at 72nd and South Prairie. Bos had his hat on. He pulled it down low so the other man could not see the color of his skin. Bos threw a pack of cigarettes at the man. "Have a smoke," Bos said. As the man caught the pack, Bos slipped the noose over his head and got behind the man, tightening with the two-hand motion. He was a small man. Athletic. He struck over the shoulder with his left hand while simultaneously striking low and backward with his right hand. He jerked Bos forward, causing him to lose his balance. Bos fell on top of the man. As he went down, he drove both forearms into the back of the man's neck. The crunching sound told him what had happened. The body was limp. The man was dead. There was no time to waste. He sprinted the half block to the Capone house.

Earlier in the day, he had pried open the ground-level window on the side of the house. He pushed it open and eased himself through the window feetfirst.

He knew the two men inside would be on heightened alert. The two spokes had not returned to the hub. That was a problem. Bos ascended the stairs, walking near the far end of each stair to avoid the creaking. As he approached the top step, he could see one man sitting at the table. Beer bottle in hand. Looking straight at him. Bos would have smiled if time permitted. This black apparition coming out of the basement.

The Counterattack

Bos barreled at the man. There was no time for the garrote. He flew over the table at the man's head. Both men landed hard on the floor behind. Bos had to give Capone credit. He had picked a number of young, athletic men. Fischetti rolled away from Bos. He pulled out a .38 revolver six-inch from the left cross-draw holster. The shot was deafening. It went wide. Bos moved at the man. His best shot was going to be going straight at him. No time for a firearm. With his full force, he sprung at the man at a 45-degree angle. He drove his head straight into Fischetti's jaw. The head snapped back. Bos pulled his Ka-Bar from his left pant leg and drove the blade under the man's breastbone straight into the heart with a twisting motion. One down and one more to go.

Bos could hear the footsteps on the stairway. It sounded like two heavy men coming down the stairs. He picked up Fischetti's .38 and fired at the lead man moving toward the front door. The bullet hit the man's right arm. He turned directly at Bos, smiled, and charged. There was no time for a second shot. He came straight at Bos. He was smaller than Bos. He came in low like a middle linebacker. Bos let go of the .38. The two men fell to the floor. Both grappled to get on top of the other. The other man was up first and threw his right knee at Bos's midsection. Bos doubled over. Bos drove the heel of his right hand into the man's face. The sound of bone giving way on impact was something Bos had heard before. Even with the distorted face, Bos could tell this man was the brother of the man he had just killed.

The Fischetti boys knew how to spar. Bos could hear the car engine in the driveway firing up. Capone was the prize. Survival was on the plate at the moment. Fischetti came straight at him. His left jabs were quick. Bos's longer reach kept him at a distance. The man had an intensity about him that said the jabs were the prelude.

Fischetti kicked some of the furniture out of the way to open up the floor area. He dropped to the floor on his left hand and did a sweeping kicking motion with his right foot. He impacted Bos's left calf. Bos fell to the floor. Fischetti was on top of him this time with a nine-inch knife in his left hand. Bos could see the gleaming metal coming straight at his throat.

In Northern France, Bos had learned to admire the marines who fought with abandon. They also fought with leather collars around their necks. Bos and his brothers had developed their own versions of leather necks. The knife hit the two-inch strip of leather and got stuck.

Bos grabbed the knife handle, pulled it out of the leather, and brought the knife handle back at the man's left clavicle. He rolled off Bos screaming.

The clavicle would never be the same.

Bos got to his feet and ran for the door. Capone was gone. He needed to check on how his own brothers were faring with Torrio.

Chapter Fourteen

Motorcycle Madness
August 27, 1921
Chicago, Illinois

"How did you get three Indians?" Thomas asked.

"It wasn't easy," Bos replied. "The hard part was ridin' all three of 'em back east to Chicago."

"Who helped you?" Nevin asked.

"I did it myself. Three trips. All for you," Bos smiled.

"The Indian is a great bike. What did they say when they saw a Black man tryin' to buy three of 'em?"

"As Mom used to say, they were tongue-tied. Couldn't believe I could ride a bike. Further couldn't believe I could pay for it. Reminds me of when Pops said he bought his first horse. Of course it was just a draft horse. The white man couldn't believe Pops could ride. Couldn't believe Pops had the money to pay for it either," Bos said.

"Things never change," Nevin said.

"That ain't so. Everything changes. You know that. The only thing that's constant is change; the Buddha said that," Bos said.

"Aw. Oh. Here we go again. Another lesson on spiritualism?" Thomas asked.

"No. Just a lesson on common sense."

They kept the three motorcycles in a garage in South Chicago. Bos had bought them over a year ago. He had gone out to the Indian plant in Iowa and purchased all three. The bikes were identical. He and his brothers were used to driving motorcycles in West Virginia. It was an easy way to inspect the 4,000 acres their father owned. The Indians were larger than what they had used in West Virginia. But at least here in Chicago the roads were smoother and more predictable.

"Torrio's got a big shipment leavin' today from his other warehouse. What we burned up yesterday was just a small part of his enterprise," Bos said.

"So how many trucks in this caravan?" Nevin said.

"Over 100."

"And I suppose we're gonna be shootin' out tires today?" Thomas asked.

"No. Same M.O. Hand grenades. This time, German-made. I've got over 200 of them, and we'll each take a satchel of about 40. The trucks are all open in the back. We'll set up three starting points. Thomas will take the lead and pick up the caravan at the end of the first 30 trucks. Throw the hand grenade in the back of the truck and move on to the next one. Remove the cap on the handle and pull the cord. You've got 4.5 seconds. Just throw it and move. Nevin, you pick up at truck number 60. I'll take the back 40. If your aim is any good, this should go quickly and destructively," Bos said.

"Sometimes I think you're a dreamer. A dreamer who never wakes up," Nevin said.

"You're right. I never want to wake up."

Bos had stored over 200 of the German contact grenades in the garage. He gave 40 of the grenades to each of his brothers. He took 50.

The caravan was scheduled to leave Torrio's other warehouse at 8:00 a.m. Bos knew the route it would be following. The three brothers stationed themselves at intersections far enough apart that they could begin their destruction at about the same time. Bos set off the first grenade. The German-made grenades exploded with devastation. They were easier to throw than were the egg-shaped American grenades. Bos

The Counterattack

had learned to like German technology. Mauser rifles had a better sighting system than the Springfield. After all, the Springfield was copied from the Mauser.

Bos picked up the rear of the caravan shortly after 8:00 a.m. The first truck he hit had no forewarning. Some of the trucks had a man riding shotgun. Most did not. The hand grenade blew away the back of the truck. Bos could see the driver open the door and jump out. The truck was on fire. He sped up to the next truck and threw his grenade. This driver was not so lucky. The exploding bottles burned up the driver's cab.

In less than 10 minutes, he had blown up his 40 trucks.

Chapter Fifteen

Union Rumble
August 27, 1921
Harpers Ferry, West Virginia

Fancy Hart was a sight to behold. Six feet eight and 300 pounds. He took a fancy to getting out of tight places in the mines. He got down off the draft horse he was riding. He was winded. The horse was winded. Tough to tell who was breathing harder.

Hart was surprised to see a man on the porch who was his size.

Cookie Custer was six feet five and 280 pounds. Born in Alabama. He freed himself from slavery in 1863 and headed north to fight with the man who gave him his name, George Armstrong Custer. Cookie knew that the arrival of Fancy Hart meant more problems at the mine in West Virginia.

"Don't even start to tell me why you're here," Cookie bellowed. "Hasn't my son done enough?"

"You must be the dad," Hart said.

"You know who I am just like I know who you are. We've never met. But we know each other. I don't dislike you. I just don't want you comin' around here askin' my sons to do your biddin'."

"This time it's a little different. We're not asking for help for us. It's other miners down in the southern part of West Virginia. They need his help. Blair Mountain down in Logan County is about to blow. The owners at Blair Mountain have brought in their own police force. The miners outnumber the goons, but the goons have bigger weapons. We know Bos has weapons. We know that he can use them. Both he and his weapons would be put to good use."

"Same story different setting."

"No sir. Different story. Different setting. Blair Mountain is like nothing we've seen. When it blows, there will be hundreds of miners killed. They mostly white men. But we all do the same job. White or black, at the end of the day we're all black. Bos knows that. That's part of the reason he's helped us before. We know he's got Lewis guns. We know he's got Thompsons. We don't want to use them, but we know without them these miners don't have a chance."

"OK. I don't like it. I don't like it one bit. But I'll let you talk to my son. I already know what he'll do. But you make your pitch to him and maybe, maybe for once he'll give his family priority. Not all these causes that he seems to want to chase are worthy."

Cookie walked back into the house. He shouted over the shoulder, "There's a pitcher of lemonade on the table. Help yourself, Mr. Fancy Hart."

Chapter Sixteen

Sturmtruppen
June 5, 1918
Northern France

Sturmtruppen. Storm troopers. Bos and his brothers knew them well. They had tried to copycat their tactics. Copycat was never good enough for Bos. He had to do them one better. He had not only adopted their principle of surprise, but he also struck only at night. Only struck the rear lines. And struck with a small force of three men. He and his two brothers.

Now the French had learned of a planned storm trooper attack by the Germans.

Bos and his brothers had been asked to intercept the German storm troopers and to meet them head-on.

Bos had no intention of meeting them head-on. He knew that would be fatal. He recognized that man-for-man these Germans might be better soldiers. They had been fighting in the trenches and on the battlefield for more than three years. They were hardened. They were fearless. They thought they were invincible. They may have been.

The aerial intelligence that Bos had received through the French was that these German storm troopers were going to attack a French battalion from the south. They intended to hit the rear supply lines to try to break the lines.

Bos decided that rather than attacking head-on, he would hit the storm troopers at their rear flank. He knew the belly of the beast was always a soft spot.

The Counterattack

Bos liked to travel light. This time he violated that rule. He and his two brothers had backpacks that were filled with ammunition for their Lewis guns. They were each carrying about 30 to 40 pounds of ammunition. The Lewis gun weighed 28 pounds. It was 50 inches long and 4.5 inches wide with a barrel length of 26 inches. It could accommodate a .30-06 round. The same as the Springfield. It could fire 500 rounds a minute.

The Germans never knew what hit them. Bos and his brothers ran at the rear element of the German storm troopers. The weight of the Lewis guns and the ammunition slowed them down. They got within 30 yards of the rear element of the German storm troopers. They opened fire, shooting high above the rear troops and aiming for the troops that were in the lead. The Custers then brought their fire down, focused on the rear element. They each fired five of the magazines. That meant that each of them had fired about 300 rounds. Almost 1,000 rounds total. That was a lot of lead.

Each of them reloaded and then ran at the Germans.

Firing the gun on the run was not easy. The weapon gave off heavy vibrations. The barrel on each gun was red-hot. Bos and his brothers had each doubled up on gloves to allow them to handle the barrel.

A German officer staggered toward the Custers. "Who are you?"

"We're the Custers. American-made. America bound."

Chapter Seventeen

Mountain Siege
August 30, 1921
Logan County, West Virginia

It took almost three days for Bos, Thomas, Nevin, Jack Jackson, Tommy Johnson, Hiram Washington, and Fancy Hart to drive to Mingo County in the southwestern part of West Virginia. Fancy Hart had a vehicle to himself because of his size. His vehicle also carried twelve Thompsons and four Lewis guns.

Bos had left a very unhappy Lee Ann behind. She couldn't understand why he was traveling several hundred miles to help men he did not know.

When they arrived, Bos began to wonder why he had left the peace of Harpers Ferry to travel to this land of uncontrolled violence. From the mine at Lady Monica, Bos had learned about the company town system. It was a repressive system. The company issued scrip as the currency for the miners. They could only use it at company stores. The mine owners had been successful in keeping unions out of the area. Intimidation was the tactic.

The owners used detectives to harass and control the miners and to identify any troublemakers. Any that the detectives identified were evicted from the company homes. The Baldwin-Felts detective agency had been in the forefront of the head bashing.

A local sheriff by the name of Sid Hatfield had attempted to protect the miners from the detectives. On August 1, 1921, Sheriff Hatfield had been gunned down by Baldwin-Felts detectives.

The Counterattack

Bos knew that many of the miners were World War I veterans. Some of the men were Black. The vast majority were white.

In response to the assassination of Sheriff Hatfield, thousands of the miners began a march from Logan County to Mingo County to confront the owners and to free miners who had been imprisoned there. The detectives were led by Sheriff Don Chafin of Logan County.

When Bos arrived, there were nearly 10,000 union men lead by a Baptist minister and miner by the name of John Wilburn.

Pastor Wilburn was inspecting some of the Springfield rifles. Some of the men were armed with shotguns. He told all the men, "It's time to lay down the Bible and take up the rifle." And he knew how to use a rifle.

When the union men arrived at Blair Mountain, they were almost 10,000 strong. Sheriff Chafin had gathered about 3,000 men of his own. They were state police, deputies, and citizen militia. Blair Mountain was en route to the miners' destination in Mingo County. The sheriff and his troops had set up an elaborate defense around Blair Mountain. The mountain itself was 2,000 feet high. Most of the defenses were near the top. They consisted of machine gun nests and trenches.

Bos and his brothers had seen this before. Bos offered Pastor Wilburn some advice.

"Aren't you Bos Custer?" cried out one of the voices.

"I am indeed. Who are you?" Bos said.

"I am one of the guys who drank a lot of the beer you stole from the Germans one night."

"I thought you guys might've forgotten about that."

"No such luck. The guys in our unit who are here still talk about you. We'll follow you anywhere, Bos. You give the order. Pastor, you need to step aside and let that fighting man lead."

Pastor Wilburn stepped forward. He was a short man. Not more than five feet nine. Boxy. A shortly cropped beard speckled with gray. The intense eyes said this was a man on a mission. Bos knew he was not a man to be trifled with.

"You men know Mr. Custer. I don't. What I know is you. You say Mr. Custer should lead this crew, then I say Mr. Custer should lead this crew. Let's say a prayer that the good Lord will lead this man. Will lead our union. Will give us the basic rights to a fair wage and safe working conditions."

Bos and his brothers looked at each other. They were all waiting for the shoe to drop. How were these three Black men going to lead this ragtag army? They didn't know. What they did know was they needed to gather intelligence as to where the enemy was and how they were dug in.

Bos asked the pastor to identify the men who had been the leaders. There were 10 of them. Three of them had Springfield rifles. One had a Mauser. The other six had 22 rifles or shotguns.

Bos looked at the Mauser and said, "Northern France?"

"Yessir."

"No officers on deck here. You can call me Bos. We'll just go by last or first names. If you don't know my two brothers, they are Thomas and Nevin. We all fought together in France. What we need is information. Where are they dug in and how? What weapons do they have, and what is their range? I need men who know Blair Mountain and know the woods. It is almost dark. I need your six best men for reconnaissance. Can you have 'em here in 30 minutes?"

"Done," one of the men responded.

The six men who showed up smelled of coal dust.

"I take it you know this mountain. I don't. I need you to be my eyes. I need to know where the sheriff's men are dug in and the weapons they

The Counterattack

have. We'll break up into three groups of three. My brothers and I will be the third man in each group. I'd prefer you leave any long barrel weapons here. Too much chance of reflection. If you don't have a side arm, then take the long barrel. Keep it by your side to reduce the chance of reflection. We can't afford to be spotted. We know they're on this side of the mountain. You need to tell me the best way up and the best way to see their positions."

"That's easy, Bos. There's an old logging trail on the far side of the mountain over there. We can follow that up to about 1,500 feet. From there we can split up. They are probably dug in below that level," one of the men said.

"What's your name?"

"Jenkins. They call me Jenks."

"Jenks, you lead the way. Spread out in staggered formation. Keep your long rifles on the downhill side of your body. No talkin'. Walk on your toes and try to make no noise."

Jenks was right. It was an old logging trail. At least it was old. It was covered with weeds knee-high. They moved slowly uphill. After an hour of marching, Jenks called a halt. "I figure we're at about 1,500 feet. If they dug in, they probably dug in below us."

"It looks like the trail forks here. I say we send one group on the left fork up higher and the other two groups to the right lookin' for their positions," Bos said.

"I agree," Jenks said.

"We meet back here in two hours."

One group proceeded to the left uphill. The other group proceeded to the right. The group Bos was with stayed put for 15 minutes listening to the sounds of the forest.

"I can hear 'em down there. Hear the rustlin' of the pans?" Bos asked. "Sounds like they're cookin' dinner. An army eats quietly. No pans. No talk. No fires. See the small fire about 300 yards over that way?"

"You got good eyes, first sergeant," one of the men said.

"One of us needs to get closer to that fire. They think that because the fire is covered that people can't see it. Any of you experienced hunters?" Bos asked.

"We both are. But I am a little lighter on my feet than Wechsel here. I'll go out."

Twenty minutes later, the hunter returned. "They've got a machine gun emplacement. They're well dug in. This would be Northern France all over again if we charge up this mountain."

"That's what I need to know. We won't be charging up the mountain."

An hour later, the other two groups reported back. Multiple machine gun emplacements.

"They must have figured Blair Mountain could stop us. What they didn't know was we brought some potato mashers."

"Potato mashers. How does that help us?" Jenks asked.

"German grenades," Nevin said. "Easy to throw, and they blow on contact."

Sheriff Chafin knew the landscape. But Bos now had a plan.

Chapter Eighteen

The Mashers
September 1, 1921
Logan County, West Virginia

"Where the devil did you get these?" Jenks asked.

"We were the last ones to come back from Northern France. They put us on a segregated boat. No questions asked of what we carried. No questions asked about what we had in the footlockers. I had three footlockers filled with these grenades. No one cared. I kept 'em dry and high in a shed in West Virginia. I tested some of 'em on the way down here. They still work," Bos said.

"Guys always said you were creative. I believe it."

"These are percussion grenades, not fragmentation. They don't shoot out shrapnel. They just dig a deeper hole. Five seconds from the time the cord is pulled. I have 10 vests. The grenades fit in the loops in the front and back. We'll give each man 12 of the grenades. Once you've blown out the entrenched areas, just use the grenades to cause havoc. We're not attackin' the entrenched positions. We're just tryin' to destroy them," Bos said to the assembled men.

"Bos, do they explode on impact?" one of the men asked.

"Five seconds after you pull the cord. The first group of three follows the trail where we came from for one mile. Try to spread out as much as you can to hit as many emplacements as possible. The second group follows the trail one half mile and does the same thing. The three of us will go down about 100 yards. Group one fires first. Once we hear those blasts, we all let go of our grenades. Happy huntin'."

At 2:00 a.m., the first group moved out. The three of them were experienced hunters. They knew where to step. They knew how to step. They kept their weapons away from the overhead moonlight. Bos wished he'd had men like this in Northern France.

The first explosions came about 30 minutes later. There was a rapid succession. The second group of explosions followed. Bos gave the signal to his team to move out. He took the furthest assignment. He knew he could throw a grenade 40 to 50 yards. The low-hanging branches were an obstruction. He unleashed the first grenade from a distance of about 30 yards from the machine gun emplacement. He could see the explosion light up the gun and knock it over. The men in the trenches stood up dazed. None of them had suffered fatal wounds. The percussion deafened all of them. Bos got to his knees and threw three more grenades. From the kneeling position, he had a chance of avoiding the low-lying branches. The men in the trenches who could move ran down the hill. The miners at the bottom of the hill could hear them coming. They shouted out the password. There was no response from the detectives. The miners began firing. At least 30 detectives were killed that evening.

When Bos and his eight men returned to the base, they were greeted with applause.

"No time for celebration. These men are well armed and well trained. They may be outnumbered. But keep in mind our forces are no match for these trained killers. Get some sleep now. Guard duty will rotate every hour on the hour."

Chapter Nineteen

Aerial Attack
September 2, 1921
Logan County, West Virginia

Brigadier General Billy Mitchell had volunteered for the opportunity. He knew that Sheriff Chafin had plans of dropping bombs from his biplanes. Mitchell wanted nothing to do with that. He wanted to test the effectiveness of aerial reconnaissance. His planes flew over the countryside. They were able to locate the miners and map their movement. Bos had no idea that one of the pilots he saw overhead was Mitchell.

Chafin had chartered three biplanes. Equipped them with tear gas and pipe bombs. The bombs were loaded with nuts and bolts. Nasty shrapnel. In the morning at 8:00 a.m., the miners awoke to the sound of Chafin's planes. The bombs they dropped were pushed over the gunwales of the planes by the pilot. Their accuracy was close to zero. None of the shrapnel hit the miners. Some of the tear gas blew their way.

Bos took aim at one of Chafin's planes. He knew if he hit the pilot, the plane might take a nosedive into a group of miners. He aimed at the engine to disable the plane and give it a chance of landing. With his Springfield, he was able to put two rounds into the engine of the lead plane. He saw it begin to smoke. Even with no engine, the plane had enough speed to glide at least a couple of miles. The other two planes quickly left the area.

"I heard on the radio that President Harding has ordered 2,000 troops to the area. You know a lot of the men are veterans. They don't want to shoot at the troops," Jenks said.

"I can understand that. My brothers and I don't want to do that either. I understand the preacher led his own assault yesterday," Bos said.

"Yep. A disaster. Nothing but disaster. The men walked straight into two machine gun nests. Over 50 wounded or killed. The preacher needs to stick with preaching."

"I don't know how much more we can do for you here, Jenks. I know many of you men have families. I have a family. I need to get back to them. I think what we did last night set the owners back. It looks like the owners aren't gonna tuck tail and run."

"I understand Bos. You and your brothers are good men. We appreciate what you did. Fancy, you're welcome to stay. We can use all the help we can get," Jenks said.

"Thanks, Jenks. I only got one way home. That would be with Bos. I better take it," Fancy said.

Bos extended his hand to Jenkins. They looked each other in the eye and thought the same thing. *Large groups of stupid people are very dangerous.*

Chapter Twenty

Four Deuces
September 5, 1921
Chicago, Illinois

It was Torrio's flagship. The address, 2222 S. Wabash Avenue, gave it its name: the Four Deuces. Restaurant. Bordello. Brewery. Gambling casino. Capone was in charge of all four. Torrio was becoming more and more reliant on Capone. Capone had a head for numbers. For a sixth-grade dropout, he could manage numbers in his head better than anyone Torrio had ever seen. Torrio was not afraid to ask his accountants and bookkeepers for help. He felt more comfortable asking Al. He got straight answers. If Al didn't know the answer, he found it.

The club was in the Levee District. South Chicago was becoming a battle zone. As Torrio tightened the grip, there was more and more resistance. Newspaper headlines told the story of gang warfare. Capone knew there was a price on his head. Also on his boss's head.

The four-story building was unimpressive. One floor was for whoring. One floor was for gambling. All of the floors were for boozing. It was not a standalone building, so there was sunlight only at the street front and at the rear.

The Custers had only done limited reconnaissance of the building. They were able to enter from the adjoining building. They went up to the rooftop of that building and walked over to the rooftop of the Four Deuces.

Nevin was the first to enter. Bos and Thomas held the rope while Nevin lowered himself down to the fourth-floor window. He swung out from the brick facing and swung through the fourth-floor window. It wasn't pretty. It was noisy. But the room was empty. Nevin got up off the floor and went to the door. At 6:00 a.m., he wasn't expecting any traffic. He exited and looked for the doorway to the roof. It was in the corner of the building. The door was unlocked. He went through the door and closed it behind him. There was a circular stairway that led up to the roof. When he got to the top, he knocked. The knock was returned. He opened the door.

"What took you so long?" his older brother asked.

"A few panes of glass and somethin' called a window," Nevin said.

"I hope they're all asleep," Thomas said.

"Not for long," Bos said. "Open as many windows as you can. I hope you two remember how to throw a football."

"You might remember Pops always said two of us had a better arm than you did," Nevin hurled back at him.

"Just keep in mind we're runnin' out of grenades. I might have to send one of you back to Germany to get some more."

"No way you gettin' us anywhere near that country," Thomas replied.

Nevin and Thomas went down to the fourth floor.

As they ran down the hallway, they opened every door they passed, peeked in, and then went in and opened the windows. Back at street level, Bos handed out three grenades to each of his brothers. "You know what we're doin'. You two go in the back. I'll stay in the front. Fire at will."

The two brothers ran to the left to the end of the block to get behind the building. Bos didn't wait. He pulled out the first grenade and threw it up to the fourth floor. To his amazement, it went through the open window. What was left of the window blew out. Bos could only guess what happened to the nearby walls. Twenty seconds later, he heard the explosion from the rear of the building. He had never doubted the ability of his two brothers to hit a target they were throwing at.

Bos had run out of targets. It was time to go home. Any more targets that might exist would wait another day.

Chapter Twenty-One

King George
September 6, 1921
Harpers Ferry, West Virginia

"George Armstrong Custer, don't you dare do that."

"It's not loaded," Bos said to his wife.

"I don't much care if it is loaded or not. I want him to know he does not touch a gun."

"Someday he will. You know that. No reason not to start now."

Lee Ann went over to the Winchester rifle and picked it up. She opened the action to see if there was a round in the chamber. Empty. She knew it was. She had checked it just hours before. She had meant to put the gun up. Out of reach. She hadn't. She scolded herself for not being more careful. She certainly knew the consequences. Friends and neighbors had all experienced childhood gun accidents. Safety and prevention were the only defense.

"I know. I know all about *someday*. Someday he will fire a rifle. Someday he'll fire every rifle just like you did. Let's just make sure that when that someday comes, either you or I are standin' next to him."

Bos walked over to where little George was standing. He scooped him up with his right arm. "You rascal. You got me in trouble with your mommy. I won't forget that."

Bos tossed the little boy up in the air. He was only airborne for a second. The tight curls on his head wafted upward. They had let his hair grow out. Bos smiled. The hair was nothing like the long blond hair of the cavalry officer he was named after. He squatted down and

The Counterattack

let the little boy jump on his back. George held on tight while his father grabbed his legs from behind.

"I'll be back in time for dinner."

"You better be. No gunplay with my baby."

"Just play. Nothing more."

Bos walked toward the stairs. "You need to get down, little man, so we can go down the stairs safely." Bos squatted down until the boy could drop to the floor on his feet. He took his hand and together they walked down the stairs to the front door.

Bos wanted to inspect the defenses. He felt Capone had had enough of West Virginia warfare. Torrio was tiring of the Chicago mayhem. There was no peace. Business was booming but still no peace. No peace at all. No peace without vigilance.

Bos Custer had become an embarrassment for Capone. This small-time hustler had destroyed hundreds of Torrio's trucks. Spooked all of his men with the use of the garrote. Driven a wedge between Torrio and Capone. Torrio had said, "Give him a piece. Make peace." Capone was thinking there was no logic in fighting Torrio on this. He knew what Bos wanted: control of the market from Baltimore to Florida. That was a small carve-out.

Bos knew there would be no carve out. No peace. As he exited the front door of the house, he admired the tall radio antenna he had installed in the front yard. It was tall enough to pick up the signal from Pittsburgh. KDKA was a 50,000-watt nondirectional transmitter of radio waves that could be picked up even in West Virginia with the right antenna. The world was changing. He and Lee Ann together had heard Harding's inauguration speech sitting in their home in West Virginia. Just weeks earlier they had heard the baseball game from Forbes Field in Pittsburgh. It was the Pittsburgh Pirates versus the Philadelphia

Phillies. He couldn't even remember the score. All he knew was the world was changing rapidly. His little boy needed to be prepared.

Chapter Twenty-Two

Black Bottom
September 7, 1921
Harpers Ferry, West Virginia

"Why not?" Bos asked.

"I don't know how to do it," Lee Ann said.

"I'll teach you. It's all over the radio. Everybody's doin' it."

"What's it called again?"

"The Black Bottom."

"You seem to know so much about it. Why don't you dance by yourself?" Lee Ann asked.

Bos and Lee Ann had invited all of the workers into their home for dinner. They wanted to celebrate the end of summer and a successful growing season. Some of the men had brought their instruments. They set up a quartet in the corner of the large room.

Bos, ever the teacher, walked to the center of the room. "Some people say it started in the South. I think it started in Detroit in a part of town known as Black Bottom. Say what you want. It's a crazy dance. A little bit like the Charleston."

The dance moves started slowly. As the name implied, it involved a lot of hip motion. Bos had the moves. He kept looking at Lee Ann. She came onto the dance floor. In no time, her gyrations were every bit as suggestive as his. They laughed at each other. The men gathered around and clapped. Cookie was the first to join in. In no time, he brought Rhonda in. Nevin, not to be outdone by his father, joined in. Before long, the house was shaking.

The quartet tired before the dancers.

"I ain't seen you have that much fun in years," Thomas said to his father.

"I haven't *had* that much fun in years. Your mother and I loved dancin'. Sometimes we would just dance alone. No music. No singin'. No melody. Just the two of us," Cookie said.

"I believe it. I remember as a boy seein' the two of you dancin'. We used to wonder what you were doin'. The two of you just loved bein' alone. She loved bein' in your arms."

"I loved pickin' her up. She was like a little waif. She had an appetite like a full-grown man, but she never put on any weight. I guess she just burned it all up. Constant motion. Made no difference whether she was in the house, in the classroom, or in the backyard. She was movin'. I miss everything about her. But I miss the motion the most. Just not the same anymore."

Calpurnia had been gone for more than 10 years. Bos, Thomas, and Nevin could all tell their father thought about her every day. Every day. Every minute of every day.

Chapter Twenty-Three

Ruth Might Hit 60
September 8, 1921
Harpers Ferry, West Virginia

"He just might. He just might make it 60. I think he's right around 50 now," Cookie said.

"How do you know all this stuff?" Rhonda asked.

"Haven't you been listenin' to the radio? Bos has us tuned in. I know what's goin' on in the world. I'm becomin' a man of the world."

"I won't fall for that. You're still stuck in the Civil War. I can't blame you. You were young then. Happy days."

"Hardly happy. But they were different. For a Black man to wear a Union uniform with three hard stripes meant somethin'. It meant more than somethin'. It meant a whole lot," Cookie said.

"I overheard that. Ruth is not at 50 yet. He's close," Bos said.

"Well, he's right close to 50," Cookie said.

"You do know your baseball. Maybe we should build a small diamond in front of the house. We'll see what you're really made of. I know you can throw a football. But can you hit a baseball?" Bos said.

"We got plenty of flatland in front of this house. I'd suggest maybe you and your brothers smooth out the surface and we can play a little game this evenin'. 6:00 p.m. Just before sunset. It'll be Nevin and me against you two."

"Maybe I'll ask some of the other boys to join in. I think some of them have played ball. We'll see what you're made of. 6:00 p.m. sharp," Bos said.

The rest of the day Bos, Nevin, and Thomas spent their time grooming the infield, marking the obstructions in the outfield, and setting up some seating along the baselines.

By the time 5:00 came, the field had been nicely groomed. Thanks to the Custer brothers.

At 6:00 p.m. sharp, Cookie called out, "Any ground rules?"

"Lots of ground rules. The fans must stay on the first base side behind the nettin'. The bags are filled with hay. They're not tied down. The outfield has some pop-up holes. So be careful. Have fun," Bos said.

The first pitcher was Joe Taylor. At five feet eight and 200 pounds, he was not the model of a pitcher. They only had three baseballs. Cookie couldn't remember where they had come from or how old they were, but they had some age on them.

Taylor had played baseball as a young man. He was a catcher. Even though he threw from the shoulder, he had velocity. They found a total of 14 players. Seven players per side: two outfielders, three infielders, and a battery.

Bos was the first batter. Taylor had the advantage after two pitches. It was 0–2. Bos stepped away from the plate. The plate was just a square piece of plywood. He looked at Taylor and said, "You're not gonna get me."

Taylor smiled.

The next pitch was a curveball. Cookie stood 10 feet behind the pitcher. He had his own catcher's glove as protection. He punched his son out. Third strike. One out. Bos was embarrassed. He looked at his father. His father stared back and walked at him.

"Don't you dare challenge my call. That was a beautiful pitch. A sight to behold." Cookie smiled and walked back to his umpire's position.

Chapter Twenty-Four

Third Inning
September 9, 1921
Harpers Ferry, West Virginia

It was the bottom of the third inning. Joe Taylor was batting. Thanks to his solid pitching, the score was tied at 2–2.

Bos saw Taylor fall. Then he heard the crack of the rifle. The shooter had to be more than 1,000 yards away. A marksman. Bos thought of Jackie Franco. The marine veteran. A rock climber. A marksman, Franco had told Bos that he had spent time in the European mountains fighting the Germans. He had honed his marksmanship skills in targeting German officers.

Bos cried out one word, "Attack." All the men knew what that meant. "Pops, get everybody inside. You know what to do."

Bos ran to Taylor. It had been a perfect shot. Center of mass. Taylor was dead. There was nothing more Bos could do for him.

He ran to the house to get his Springfield. Thomas and Nevin were with him. "I think it's Franco. That shot was probably 1,000 yards given the delay in hearin' it. He's probably with Donovan. They have us in a crossfire. I'll go north after Franco. You two head southeasterly. Donovan should be somewhere in that direction. Check the promontory overlookin' the stream just before the holler."

Bos thought he knew where Franco's shot came from. He headed north. He knew Franco would be on the move. Shoot and scoot. He'd been taught by the same people who had taught Franco.

Bos knew that area of the forest. A good sniper would always head to higher ground. He decided he would try to beat Franco to the plateau that overlooked his shooting position. That meant he had to circle wide to the west. The terrain there was rugged and rocky. Bos wasted no time.

In fifteen minutes, he had positioned himself at the plateau. He heard the trudging feet. The man had let himself get out of shape. Big mistake. When the man was fifteen feet away, Bos came out from behind the tree. "Here I thought it was Franco. I didn't know you could make a shot like that."

"I've been working on it since we got home from France. In the mountains, Franco did most of the shooting. I did the spotting. I'm pretty good with windage," Ray Donovan said.

"You should be proud of yourself. Except now you're going to die. You killed my friend, Joe Taylor. He was in France. He fought with us. Army not marines. A good man. Now he's gone. I should kill you like a dog. But I'm gonna do it slowly. You tell me what your pleasure is."

"I prefer hand-to-hand." Donovan dropped the sling of the Springfield from his shoulder and let it fall to the ground. He removed the web belt around his waist.

"How about the knives?"

"I never cared much for them. Franco was big on knives."

Bos heard the rustling in the distance. He raised the .45 and fired one round to his left. Franco had just stepped out from behind a tree. The round hit him in the breastbone. Bos couldn't see the look on his face. As a marksman, he would've appreciated the precision.

"I thought the two of you would've put us in a crossfire. I guess you outsmarted me. You knew I would send my brothers in the other direction. Two against one. I figured you were better than that."

"We knew your reputation. Franco thought he could take you alone. I knew I couldn't. I'd gotten to be the better shot. So, he let me take it. He was the backup."

The Counterattack

"Unfortunately, you won't be reportin' back to Capone. You and the backup are dead men."

Bos approached Donovan. He kept the .45 ready. "Up against the tree."

Donovan turned around and leaned up against the tree. He spread his legs. Bos did a pat down looking for other weapons. None found. He pulled the slide back on the .45 to unchamber the round. He threw the handgun in one direction and the clip in the other. He kicked the man's legs out from under him. "Let the games begin."

Donovan was predictable. He sprung off the ground and came straight at Bos, running like a sprinter out of the blocks at a 45-degree angle. Bos came at him at a lower angle, aiming for the knees. Both men landed on the ground. They sprung up. Donovan came straight at Bos, a left jab extended. Bos was starting to like this guy. They thought alike. There was no such thing as a fair fight. There were just winners and losers. They had all learned that in Northern France. Bos dropped down onto his left hand and did a sweeping kick. Donovan looked like the wind had been taken out of his sails. He fell flat. Bos sprung up and jumped on top of Donovan, who was face down. First, he drove his right elbow into Donovan's right kidney. Then he drove his left elbow into Donovan's left kidney. Bos knew that would disable him for a few moments.

Donovan got to his feet. Bos came in close and drove the heel of his right hand into Donovan's face. A showstopper. Donovan staggered. Bos approached. He drove the heel of his left hand into the same spot. Donovan fell to the ground.

"Just kill me, why don't you?"

"You killed my friend. A good friend. A good man. Just to please Capone. He never fought. He brags that he did. You know he didn't. How can you work for a guy like that?"

"It's just business, Custer."

"Yep. Just business." Bos dragged him 20 yards to a precipice. The drop was at least 100 feet. "Just business, Donovan." Bos threw him off the precipice.

Chapter Twenty-Five

Wicked Witch
September 10, 1921
Harpers Ferry, West Virginia

"They won't know what hit 'em. The wicked witch from the east can deliver a powerful blow," Lee Ann smiled.

"But you're seven months pregnant. How do you do somethin' like this?" Bos said.

"Pregnancy doesn't mean I'm disabled. If anything, I am enabled. No one will suspect me."

"So, you're sayin' you can move to Chicago, organize the women in the brothels, and get them to go on strike?"

"That's what I'm sayin'. It's 1921. Women have the right to vote. I'm not sayin' the women are gonna leave whorin'. All I'm sayin' is we can organize 'em to take over the brothels. They don't need men to run the brothels. Women can run 'em, hire men for enforcement, and keep the profits for themselves. That cuts Torrio and Capone out of the business."

"You are a wicked woman!" Bos smiled. "Sometimes I like to ask myself what my mother would think."

"She'd smile. She understood the power of organized labor. I do too."

"What do you need to get started?"

"I'll leave tomorrow. The baby stays with you. That means you stay here. I'll need a ride north to get on the Pennsylvania Railroad headin' west. I'd like to take Hiram Washington and Jack Jackson with me for protection. I'll be gone a week. If I can't make inroads in that period of time, then I'll give up."

"I doubt you'll give up on anything. I'm sure you can talk many of these women into workin' with you. We can provide the muscle. Just tell 'em the muscle will all be Black. Good men who will stand their ground."

"I'm sure Hiram and Jack can convey that message," Lee Ann said.

Chapter Twenty-Six

To Harrisburg
September 11, 1921
Harrisburg, Pennsylvania

"You didn't tell me the road to Harrisburg was filled with ruts," Lee Ann said.

"You didn't ask," Bos replied.

"You got an answer for everything don't you?"

"Nope. Just the questions that are asked."

Hiram and Jack sat in the backseat. They didn't say a word. Just smiled.

Harrisburg was the capital of Pennsylvania. A river ran through it. It looked like the river ruled. High-water marks were visible on the buildings alongside the river. The business owners in the buildings had perishables stacked above water level. Nothing about the town appealed to Bos.

Bos purchased three tickets. He had ridden a train west more than once. Coloreds in the back. He wasn't sure how his wife would react to that. He didn't have to wait long.

"They sit with me," Lee Ann said to the conductor.

"Ma'am there are no exceptions. Coloreds sit in the back," said the conductor.

"These two fine gentlemen may have some different thoughts about where they sit. I think they are used to sittin' wherever they want."

Jackson and Washington opened up their coats. The .45 handguns they carried on their hips were visible. The conductor took a quick look.

"Madam, I will do everything I can to accommodate you and your guests."

Lee Ann knew that meant that he was going to get his local goons. He'd be back.

Bos stood at a distance. He smiled at the resolve his wife had shown. He knew she would not be deterred. As the train began moving, Bos saw two carloads of tough-looking men show up. The driver of each car got out and ran toward the train. Beckoning anyone to bring it to a stop. To no avail. The train did not stop. It was ever westward.

The eight men looked around. They went into the train station and sat in the café, no doubt awaiting further instructions from their handlers.

Bos knew these eight men would be no match for Hiram and Jack. He decided to do them a favor and spare them an ass whupping. He walked alongside the first car they had arrived in. His Ka-Bar sunk into the two driver's side tires. He then finished the task with the other car. He walked back toward the train station. The eight men were still enjoying their midday meal. Bos smiled.

Chapter Twenty-Seven

The New Madam
September 12, 1921
Chicago, Illinois

"You don't look like you're ready for the mattresses," the woman said.

She was about five feet six and weighed 130 pounds. She looked like she could take care of herself. She had a toughness about her. The high cheekbones, tightly drawn lips, and red hair said this was a woman who was used to being noticed. A woman who was used to giving orders. Used to having her orders followed.

"I've already done my apprenticeship. I'm lookin' to enlist women who want to protect themselves. Protect their profits and protect their bodies. Torrio and Capone won't do that," Lee Ann said.

"You're preaching to the choir. I been saying that for years. The girls won't listen. They want the protection. They want the guys with big necks close by in case something goes wrong."

"I didn't get your name," Lee Ann asked.

"They call me Sheila. My middle name is the Enforcer."

"You look like you could enforce. How about enforcin' for yourself?"

"Tell me what's in it for me and how you protect me when Torrio sends Capone around to enforce."

"We'll have a force of 20 men ready to go anywhere in the city to help. You call day or night, and we'll have 10 men on your doorstep within 10 minutes. They'll be well-armed and ready for combat."

"I'd like to see this force of 20 men. Are they on duty now? I'd like to see them. The guys that Torrio sends around all have big necks and shoulders as wide as that door."

"Our guys are mostly World War I vets. They fought in Northern France. They're still fightin'. Capone's guys will be no match for them. I can assure you. I've seen these guys in action."

Hiram went outside. On the sidewalk, he waved to the three vehicles parked at the nearby intersection. Each had six occupants. The 18 men got out of their vehicles. They were all at least the size of Hiram. Some of them were six inches taller. Big men. Big shoulders. Big guns that they knew how to use.

Sheila said she was impressed. This was a lady who didn't impress easily.

"And how quickly can they be here?"

"Ten minutes or less. Any one of these men is equal to three of Torrio's men. They love to fight. They love to mix it up. They love to win."

"You know Capone has been put in charge of the brothels. He's ruthless. He comes in here and he don't like what he sees, then I'm going to the hospital. He counts bodies in the door. He then reconciles that with the money I give him. If there's any disparity, I'm the one who's gonna take the hit. I don't care for getting batted around. That's why I left my first two men. I'm not tolerating it with a third man."

"I like your style. Are you willin' to talk to the other ladies?"

"Happy to. You know, not all the houses are run by women. Capone's trying to replace the women. He don't trust us. Can't say I blame him. He's smart enough to know that the houses that are run by women produce more revenue. So he's slowing down a bit on replacing the women. He also knows that the houses that are run by women and have speakeasies are producing the most. Liquor does reduce the inhibitions."

"He sounds like an intuitive male. Unusual," Lee Ann smiled.

Chapter Twenty-Eight

Macomb Makes 'em
September 12, 1921
Harpers Ferry, West Virginia

On September 28, 1920, Eddie Cicotte walked into the White Sox team counsel's office and confessed that he had thrown the 1919 World Series to the Cincinnati Reds. Both he and Joe Jackson admitted their involvement. They testified as to six other teammates being involved. In March 1921, all eight were indicted. A jury declared all eight not guilty of conspiracy on August 2, 1921. Later that night, they celebrated with members of the jury. The newly appointed baseball commissioner was not standing for it. He banned all eight from ever again playing baseball. None of them ever again set foot in a major league park. The "eight men out" continued playing ball as barnstormers.

The Illinois towns of Macomb and Colchester had a spirited history of competition. Part of that competition was played out on the baseball field. Each town fielded teams. They regularly played traveling Negro teams. Race made no difference. It was the game that counted.

The final game was Sunday, September 11, 1921, at 3:00 p.m. at the Macomb Fairgrounds. A large crowd was expected. None of them knew who would be on the field. Additional bleachers had been set up for the game between Macomb and Colchester. The umpire announced that the starting battery for Colchester would be Eddie Cicotte and "Kid" Standard. "Shoeless" Joe Jackson was in the lineup. He and the Black Sox players were accustomed to the jeers from the fans. The knuckleballer, Cicotte, had an arsenal of pitches, including the emery

The Counterattack

ball, the drop ball, and what he called the shine ball. With them he had won 208 major league games. Colchester's victory was never in doubt.

The Colchester Red Man baseball team won. They were the champions of McDonough County that year.

Joe Jackson, after the game, went back to his dry-cleaning business in Savannah, Georgia. Eddie Cicotte and Swede Risberg went back to Chicago to continue their barnstorming.

Lee Ann called home as she had promised. Bos answered.

"Didn't you hear about the game? It's all over the radio," Bos said.

"What game?" Lee Ann asked.

"The most famous game in baseball that no one ever heard of. The 'eight men out' played in Macomb, Illinois, outside of Chicago."

"Who cares?"

"I care. Anyone who knows the name 'Joe Jackson' cares."

Chapter Twenty-Nine

First Responder
September 13, 1921
Chicago, Illinois

"I guess we'll find out if Miss Custer can deliver," Sheila said. "Call her and tell her Capone's knocking on the door. I need her posse."

The phone call was made.

Lee Ann was in her room. She had rented three rooms in Southside Chicago. She wanted Hiram and Jack nearby. She knew that couldn't happen unless she was discreet about her choice of accommodations. Federal and 19th was not an area that Lee Ann would have chosen for herself. She knew the boarding house that she was in was really just a flop house. The parade of men in and out of the rooms said it all. Lee Ann's reservation of three rooms side by side was suspicious. Cash talked. She paid in advance. She paid more than the innkeeper could expect to otherwise make on three rooms.

As soon as she got the phone call from Sheila's assistant, Lee Ann went out into the hallway and knocked on Hiram's door. "Capone is two blocks away. You need to meet him. Make sure he understands you provide the protection."

"Miss Custer, ain't he gonna think we skimmin'?" Hiram said.

"He will. That's fine. We know we're not. He doesn't need to know. What he needs to see in the next few minutes is lots of muscle and metal. You got your hands full." She turned around and walked back to her room.

She had spent a lot of time around Hiram. He was a kind man. He supported a wife and two children who lived in Washington, DC. Bos

The Counterattack

had chosen him for the job because he was restrained and careful. He would get the job done without any grandstanding.

Lee Ann walked over to the window. In less than a minute, she saw Hiram and Jack exit the building and proceed to the warehouse across the street. Inside there were over 20 men. All of them well-armed. Hiram had given Thompsons to half of the men. The other half were each armed with two .45s and an axe handle.

Lee Ann stood by the window looking at the warehouse below. She saw the door roll open to her left. Three cars exited. Hiram drove the first car. Jack stood on the running board on the passenger side of the car. He held at shoulder level a Thompson.

Sheila had reported back to her three days earlier. She had listed more than six other houses run by women. All had agreed to become part of Lee Ann's network. All of the women had doubts as to Lee Ann's ability to deliver. Lee Ann had met with each of the women individually. None of them had made the connection between Lee Ann and Bos. If they had, none had the temerity to ask how this gorgeous white woman was married to a Black man. Lee Ann anticipated their questions. She told each of the women different, but factual, stories about she and Bos and their love affair. These were businesswomen. Hard bitten. Hardscrabble. They understood the value of a dollar. More importantly they understood the nature of men. Lee Ann had convinced all of them that she was as hard as they were.

They all knew of Bos Custer. Lee Ann had a good laugh with more than one of them when they found out that Bos was short for Boston.

Capone was on the third floor of Sheila's house when Hiram and Jack arrived.

"I want two Thompsons in the front and two in the back. Tonight, we're takin' prisoners. As you men know, normally we take no prisoners," Hiram said.

Hiram was carrying his axe handle. He approached the front door, which was blocked by two very large men. Hiram raised the axe handle and drove it into the faces of both men simultaneously. Both men fell aside. Hiram ran up the first flight of stairs. He could hear the commotion on what he thought was the top floor. He grabbed the Thompson from the man behind him. When he got to the third floor, he could not see Capone. He could hear him. Hiram fired a 20-round burst into the ceiling.

Silence.

"Capone. This house is surrounded. It is now under the protection of Bos Custer. You have two minutes to get out. I will let you and your men leave with your weapons. You are outmanned and outgunned. Bos Custer wants you dead. But he insists on doin' that himself," Hiram said.

Hiram could see the quarters on the third floor were cramped. He told three of his men to go down to the bottom of the stairs. He, Jack, and two other men stayed on the third floor. They were all armed with Thompsons. He had not seen any of Capone's men with long barrel weapons. He motioned to his three men to shoot out all of the lights on the third floor. All four of them got down on their bellies. They low-crawled in different directions into each of the rooms.

"As you enter your room, shoot high," Hiram commanded. Hiram began the firing. "Capone you don't know me, but I'm Black as the ace of spades. I ain't smiling. You ain't gonna see my teeth. The next light you'll see from me are the flashes from the muzzle of this Thompson. Stand up, and I'll let you walk out."

Hiram could hear the movement in the corner of the room.

"Capone here. We're leaving. Don't mean we won't be back. But we're leaving."

The Counterattack

Hiram got up. He walked behind Capone to the top of the stairs. He held the muzzle of his Thompson to Capone's back. They walked quietly to the first floor and out the door.

"How many more men inside?" Hiram asked Capone.

"Another five aside from the two you dropped here at the front door," Capone said.

"Tell them to come out with their hands high."

Capone complied. The other five men came out. All of them had re-holstered their weapons.

Capone looked at Hiram. "You're good. How did Custer get so many good men?"

Chapter Thirty

The Morning After
September 14, 1921
Chicago, Illinois

Hiram left five of his men at Sheila's place. He didn't think that Capone would return. No need to take chances. All five men were armed with Thompsons.

The next morning, Lee Ann knocked on Hiram's door at 6:00 a.m. "Bos enjoys a cup of coffee in the morning. I thought you might have learned from him," Lee Ann said.

"Jack is the coffee drinker. He'll be here in a minute. I can hear him rustlin' next door," Hiram said.

"I didn't want to bother you last night. I know it was a late night. How did things go with Capone?"

"Easier than I thought. Capone can stand his ground. He didn't flinch last night. But we got 'em out of the house. We left behind a couple hundred rounds of ammunition in the ceiling. We fired high, hopin' to avoid bloodshed."

"Bos said you would use your brains."

"Capone's gone. Not for long I bet. When he comes back, he'll be back with more firepower."

"A day without killin' is a day without killin'. I am in favor of that. I'll go to see Sheila this mornin'. As long as she knows she and her girls are secure, she'll stay with us. But first thing first. Your men are hungry. I need some fryin' pans, lots of bacon, lots of eggs, and lots of bread. Shouldn't be too hard to find here in the Levee. That's your job. I'll meet you over at the warehouse in an hour. I'll get the fire goin'."

Chapter Thirty-One

The Greek
September 15, 1921
Chicago, Illinois

"Your men were quite effective," Sheila said.

"I'm gonna reserve judgment on that. We had some intelligence that Capone has a girlfriend in this house. That may be why he walked away. Can you tell me about that?" Lee Ann said.

"You don't miss much, do you?" Sheila said.

"That's why I'm still alive. You haven't met my husband yet. He would've expected you to tell me about that upfront."

"That's information that's on a need-to-know basis."

"Well, I need to know. Now. Right now."

"She's a Greek girl. She's up on the third floor. Capone is quite taken with her. She dyed her hair blonde. I understand it was at Capone's request. You probably know about Mae. A nice Irish girl that Capone married in Brooklyn. She's just moved out this way with Capone. She gave birth to little Al about a month before they got married. They call him Sonny. When Mae found out about the Greek, she dyed her hair blonde. She wanted Al to know that she knew. That didn't slow him down. He comes by almost every night about the same time."

"There may be some good in that. Unlikely to be anymore gunplay at your house. Is he likely to move the Greek to a new house?"

"I don't think so. He knows the girls are loyal to one house. I found her. I've protected her. I've fed her. I introduced her to Capone. Loyalty is the only key to survival for these girls. They know that."

"Can I talk with her?"

"Sure, you can. Her English is not very good. She has reason to fear you more than she fears Capone."

Together they walked into the foyer at the base of the steps.

"Third floor, first door on the left," Sheila said.

Lee Ann proceeded upstairs. When she got to the top of the stairs she waited. She could hear no noise or movement in the Greek girl's room. She had learned from her husband to always stand to the side when knocking on a closed door. All she could hear was the occasional sound from another room of a baby whimpering.

The door opened a sliver. Lee Ann could see a blonde head.

"What you want," the blonde said.

"I wanna talk. I know you're Capone's girl."

The door shut hard.

Lee Ann didn't wait. She stood back from the door about five feet. She raised her right foot and drove it into the door next to the handle. The door bounced open. Lee Ann entered. She drew her .32 pistol from her handbag.

"I just wanna talk," Lee Ann said.

"If you know I'm Capone's girl, how could you be so stupid to break in here?"

"I'm one of the Custers. I bet there has been some pillow talk about us."

"Alphonse said the Custers were all Black."

"We are. They made one exception for me. I want you to tell Capone, you're our guest. You're welcome to stay. In fact, so welcome you can't leave. As long as Capone recognizes the new labor arrangement, you'll be safe. We provide protection for all of the houses on this list. Capone and his men don't visit these houses. We'll get a percentage of the income above current levels. That is, we get a percentage of the growth. The lady in charge pays her girls and herself. Capone gets his usual 50 percent. He just doesn't have the overhead associated with collection, protection, and enforcement. We'll bear that cost for free. I'm told Capone is good with numbers and is smart. He'll know this is a good deal. The terms are not negotiable. If I have to come back here for any problems, someone will get hurt. It won't be me."

Lee Ann turned around and left. As she passed the broken door she turned around. "You'll have a new door in about two hours."

Chapter Thirty-Two

Capone Don't Care
September 15, 1921
Chicago, Illinois

The café was two blocks from Sheila's house. She was sitting in the far corner to the left as Capone entered. The driver and one other man stayed outside. Two other men accompanied Capone into the café. Each took up stations near the front entrance.

Capone smiled as he approached the booth.

"Al, you look so sharp," she said with her Greek accent.

"I told you to call me Alphonse," he smiled.

He leaned over and kissed her on the lips. "You had a visitor the other night?"

"Yes. She was pretty scary. She had a handgun. It looked like a revolver. She left this message with me. I guess she figured I didn't understand English. I understood everything she said," she smiled.

Capone looked at the document. It was handwritten. The paper was plain white with no lines. The handwriting was very precise. The unlined paper did not detract from the drafter's ability to write in a straight line. He took a moment to read it.

"Does this say the same as what she said to you?"

"Yes, Alphonse," she smiled and squeezed his hand. Capone pulled away. He folded his arms over his chest. "Who does this broad think she is?"

"She said she was Mrs. Custer. She said you would know what that meant. She sounded like she was all business. I know I could have dropped her to the floor. I've been in a lot of fist fights. But there's no doubt in my mind she would've shot me."

"You're right. She would've shot you."

Capone looked out the window of the diner. He looked over his shoulder at the two men stationed at the door. He looked at his driver and the man riding shotgun. They were all in place. "I ought to go teach this bitch a lesson."

"Alphonse, you know that only the people who care for you will tell you the truth. This woman ain't someone to mess with. I've seen that look before. In Greece we called women like that by the Latin term *materna asina firma*. I think you know what that means."

"Mother Hardass. I don't much care about her. In 12 months, I'll own the business. Torrio wants out. His wife has had enough."

Chapter Thirty-Three

Scotch Galore
September 17, 1921
Annapolis, Maryland

"They unload them about five miles offshore. Capone is usin' boats much smaller than our liberators for the transport. He thinks they're faster and therefore better. What he doesn't know is Newton's law," Bos said.

"Put your thinkin' cap on, Thomas. We're about to get a physics lesson from brother Bos," Nevin said.

Thomas raised his hand. "Teacher Bos, is this the one about F equals MA?" Thomas asked.

"Very good, little Thomas. You must have been payin' attention. I'll tell your mother what a good student you are. Now tell me what the terms mean," Bos shot back.

"*F* stands for *force*. *M* stands for *mass*. *A* stands for *acceleration*. You taught us well. Of course, the fact that your brother and I have superior brain power is a factor too."

"We've got bigger boats and faster boats. If we have to ram them, I don't think Newton's law will be proven false," Bos said.

"Let's not talk about any rammin'," Thomas said. All three boats were lashed together and were rolling with the waves. "That looks like the trawler up ahead. We need to get to them before Capone's boats arrive."

"Let's get to it," Bos said.

The boats were untied. The brothers put the idling engines into gear, and each moved off to his pre-designated position. Bos would enter from the starboard side. Thomas would take the port side. Nevin would stay back ready with the Lewis guns.

In 30 minutes, 60 barrels of 12-year-old scotch had been loaded onto the two boats manned by Bos and Thomas. Nevin could see the boats were overloaded. They pulled up alongside each other. The three Custer brothers and the six men they had brought with them transferred 20 barrels to Nevin's boat. Less than 2,000 pounds per boat was within the limits they had been operating under.

"How do we get around the Volstead Act now, big brother?" Thomas asked. "These liquids are definitely potable."

"They're still for religious use. The Catholic Church has its wine. The Jews have their wine. Why can't we have our scotch for religious use? It uplifts the soul. Besides we're still not sellin' the liquor. We're donatin' it to our pastors," Bos said.

"You have a tongue so smooth; I almost believe you," Nevin laughed.

They unlashed the boats and headed back to Annapolis. The barrels would be loaded onto trucks and then distributed.

Chapter Thirty-Four

UA Rebels
September 19, 1921
Harpers Ferry, West Virginia

"What did you expect? He belongs to you," Lee Ann said.

"Well, I thought at least he might say goodbye," Bos said.

"No way. He's just like you and you know it. You do as you please," Lee Ann smiled.

"Well, we gotta find him. No reason he can't stay here in West Virginia. I just need to know where he is and say goodbye. I think he will miss DC."

Bos crawled under the front porch thinking the cat might be hiding there. It was a tight space. The entrance he had created for the cat was intended to keep most animals out. No sign of the cat down there.

Bos shimmied out from under the porch and sat up. His overalls were covered with dirt.

Lee Ann looked at him and smiled. "There's no length that you won't go for that cat."

"He's worth it. Just like you are."

"That won't get me to go crawlin' in these tunnels lookin' for him."

"No. I wouldn't expect that. But could you climb that tree in the distance? I think I see him up there." Bos smiled.

They both pointed at a tree in the distance. Sure enough, UA was sitting on a branch looking at them. No doubt smiling.

"I'll go talk to him. Need to tell him I'm headin' back to DC tomorrow. I thought he might want to go with me. That's his choice." Bos leaned over and kissed his wife. "Thanks for the help."

The Counterattack

Bos walked over toward the tree. He had never seen a cat come down a tree. He had seen a cat climb a tree. He knew UA was smart. In spite of his name. Bos had given the cat the name based on the Marine Corps equivalent of AWOL. Marines didn't go AWOL. They went UA, unauthorized absence.

When the cat got down to the ground, he walked over to where Bos was standing.

"Meow. Meow."

"I guess that means I'm supposed to pick you up," Bos said.

"Meow."

Bos leaned over and picked the cat up with one arm.

"You didn't need to go missin'. I understand you like it in DC. It's your home turf. This is just a little change of pace. We'll come out here on occasion. Stay a few days. Then go back to DC. DC is your home. I understand the rules."

"Your cat has more control over you than I do," the female voice said from a distance.

Bos turned and saw Lee Ann. She had her hands on her hips. A frown on her face.

"I don't get you. All I do for you, and you don't mind me. This cat shows a little bit of resistance, and you give in to his demands. You are some kind of man." She smiled and walked toward him.

Chapter Thirty-Five

The Ghurkas
August 4, 1919
Northern France

The Gurkhas were mainly from Nepal. They fought as elements of the British Army. Their signature weapon was a khukuri, a curved knife.

Their name was derived from the Gorkha Kingdom, which is in the Kingdom of Nepal.

During World War I, more than 200,000 Gurkhas served in the British Army. They suffered nearly 20,000 casualties and received almost 2,000 gallantry awards.

Bos and his brothers had been offered the opportunity to fight with the Gurkhas in Northern France. They declined. Bos had reasoned that as a frontline infantryman, he was of limited usefulness. A machine gun was too formidable a weapon.

He and his brothers had achieved distinction because of surprise and daring.

Bos decided to turn the offer around on the British and let some of the Gurkhas fight with the Custers. His only condition was that they needed to be as dark complected as he and his brothers were. The British complied.

It had been said of the Gurkhas that none of them feared death. That was true of the three Gurkha soldiers who were assigned to the Custers. Their skin was as dark as the Custers'. All three of them were smaller than the Custers. All three of them had grown up in Nepal and were accustomed to running up and down the hills of Nepal carrying what was then a full British pack that weighed 40 pounds and the Mauser

The Counterattack

rifles. They were expert marksmen. All three of them could outrun the Custers. The three of them spoke the King's English just like the Custers.

The first nighttime raid they went on was against a 100-vehicle convoy carrying German supplies to the front.

British aerial intelligence had picked up the convoy while it was still in Germany. The Custers and the three Gurkhas were given six motorcycles to ride to meet the convoy and attempt to destroy it.

When Bos heard that it consisted of 100 vehicles, he knew it would be well protected.

Bos had wondered why each of the Gurkhas carried two Mausers. What he didn't know was that these Mausers were the new 1918 T-Gewehr antitank rifles. Each rifle was designed for the sole purpose of destroying armored targets. The weapon fired a .525 caliber semi-rimmed cartridge.

These cartridges could not only penetrate the engine block of each of the trucks in the convoy but probably had sufficient velocity to cause ignition.

The Gurkha senior noncommissioned officer presented new Mausers to Bos. "First Sergeant, we have special weapons. Weapons that can penetrate the engine block of these vehicles. One round properly placed will not only disable the vehicle but may set it on fire. My men and I are excellent marksmen. We know that you are too. With the large supply of ammunition that we have, we should be able to disable this entire convoy."

Bos smiled to himself. The British officer who had dispatched these three Gurkhas to work with him must not have understood the type of weapon they had.

"Where did you get these?" Bos asked.

"Two nights ago, we raided a German armory. We recognize that these Mausers were new. They had a bigger bore, they carried a larger round. The first time we test-fired them shooting at trees, we saw that their penetration power was greater than anything we had. They could easily go through a tree that was three to four inches in diameter. Our 30 caliber rounds cannot do that."

"You guys are amazing," Bos said.

"Once we get to the convoy, I suggest that we split up and disable the lead vehicles; then the following vehicles will be easy. Like shooting fish in a barrel, as you Americans say," the Gurkha NCO said.

The joint expedition had been a raving success. All 100 plus vehicles within the convoy had been disabled. Many of them had been set on fire due to the new Mauser rounds. Some of the vehicles were actually horse-drawn. None of the animals had been killed. The wagons that had been attached to the horses had all been separated. The axles had been blown apart with the use of the Mausers. The animals were now set free. The German convoy was in total disarray.

Bos had heard about the Gurkhas, but he had no idea the fearsome fighting men they were.

Chapter Thirty-Six

The Holler People
September 19, 1921
Harpers Ferry, West Virginia

"They've been helpin' out. No question. More than once, they've come to me about people snoopin' around," Bos said.

"So why are we gonna see 'em?" Thomas asked.

"We're bringin' them four cast-iron stoves, a wagon of firewood, 100 pounds of pork that's been salted, and 12 bushels of apples. These are people who got nothing. Nothing. We help 'em out, they'll help us out."

"I wish I had you for a neighbor. I probably wouldn't have to work ever again."

"No. These people live off the land. There just ain't much on the land. They work in the coal mines when there is work. But that's not dependable income. They'll appreciate what we're givin' 'em."

Bos and Thomas continued loading the two trucks. In no time, they were finished and fired up the two vehicles.

The road down to the holler was steep. Bos had been calculating in picking the location for his house and the stills. It was a highland and also a plateau. The people in the holler were on Custer property. Bos was not about to charge them rent. They knew he could. They knew they could move on and find other property. But why bother?

The trip to the holler community took no more than 20 minutes. Most of it was spent braking to control the descent of the two trucks.

"Howdy there, Bos," the man said. He was younger than Bos but looked 10 years older.

"Howdy to you also, Jacob. We brought you some things for the cold weather."

"That's mighty nice of you. You didn't have to do that."

"Tryin' to be a good neighbor. You folks have helped us out. We want to help you."

Bos and Thomas brought their two vehicles to a stop. They walked around to the back of the trucks. They both shook hands with Jacob.

"Brought you some new stoves for the winter. Some firewood, pork, and apples."

Some other members of the small eight-household community started rambling out of their homes.

"I'm sorry I don't have a stove for every home. If some of you men can help us on the forge, we can make four new stoves in the next week. That should be a stove for every house. I'll let you folks divide up what we brought." Bos was now speaking to a gathered group of 20 people. "If you need more, we got it. I know work is sparse now. So don't be afraid to ask."

The group all nodded. Bos could tell they appreciated what he had done. They didn't know how to react to the generosity of this Black man. For most of them, Bos was the first Black man they had ever seen.

The men all came up and shook the hands of Bos and Thomas.

Bos tipped his hat to the women and walked back to the trucks with Thomas.

Chapter Thirty-Seven

Enemy for Life
September 28, 1921
Chicago, Illinois

"The houses aren't that important, Johnny," Capone said.

"That's what I started with. They got me going. They've been the cash flow source. We can't just give them up," Johnny Torrio said.

"You're always telling me to look at the big picture. Think big. Don't think small. Those are your words. I never liked them, but now I do. They're right. We're about to go big. When I say big, I mean big. You've said you want out. If you decide to leave, I'll pay you. Believe me there will be plenty here. The whore houses are just a distraction. Let 'em go."

"Now you're using my own words against me. How does that happen?"

"It happens when your words are right. You're on the mark, Johnny. I should have been listening to you all along. The coloreds and the whore houses are nothing. Chicken feed. Nothing more. The money is in the booze."

"Kid, you're just trying to use my own words against me. Sure, we look at the big picture. But the details are what have gotten me to where I am."

"When you're right, you're right. I can't argue with you. You've been in this business longer than I've been alive. You got instinct. I got emotion. You got brains. I got fists. We make a good team, but sometimes one of us has to recognize the other knows more. The other may have better sense. We work together. We feed off each other, and we help each other. That's why I'm saying let 'em go. Let the houses go. Let the coloreds go. They're just an annoyance. They ain't the prize. The prize is in those oak barrels."

"Alphonse Capone, you may be smarter than I ever thought. You may be going places I could never dream of. I can see it now."

"I'm not saying, Johnny, we forget. The coloreds are enemies for life. Someday there will be payback. Not today. We got bigger fish to catch. We got bigger bucks to make. We can do it if we keep our eye on the ball."

"On the ball. You said it, boss."

Chapter Thirty-Eight

Chicago Board
September 30, 1921
Harpers Ferry, West Virginia

"Did you hear what they did?" Bos asked.

"No, but I guess you're gonna tell me," Lee Ann said.

On May 4, 1921, the Chicago Real Estate Board voted to expel members who sold homes to Black families in white neighborhoods. The board was very clear in stating that it supported segregation in housing. The board was an association of real estate brokers in the Chicago area. It endorsed placing restrictive covenants on individual properties and neighborhoods. In no time, the communities of Hyde Park, Park Manor, South Shore, and Windsor Park were restricted so that no Black person could own property in those neighborhoods.

"So is this your next cause?"

"No. But I will keep this on my list of things to address. Nevin and I are goin' out to Chicago in about a week. We need to meet with Burke and smooth out some issues. You know he supplies most of our scotch now."

"I didn't know that. I thought he had cut you off after you blew up the factory in Canada."

"He did for a few weeks. Friendship conquers all. Burke and I fought together in Northern France. Neither one of us can stay mad at the other for very long. We saved his bacon one night in Belleau Wood. German storm troopers were out at night. About to attack his full-strength platoon. Nevin, Thomas, and I had seen what they were about to do. They had surrounded the platoon with mines. There was only one way out, and the Germans had set up two machine gunners at the exit. It would've been a bloodbath. The storm troopers set up on the opposite side of where the machine gunners were and opened fire on the platoon. We took out the two machine gunners and waved Burke and his platoon out of the encirclement. Burke made sure we got full credit for what we had done. As usual, none of the commanders wanted to hear about what the Black troops had done."

Chapter Thirty-Nine

M. L. Smith
October 7, 1921
Chicago, Illinois

M. L. Smith had been president of the Chicago Real Estate Board for years. He owned his own real estate business. He was successful. Landed. Pure bred. And not about to give any of that up to a bunch of uppity negroes who wanted to live with white people.

Bos approached the tall white man as he came out of his office building.

"Mr. Smith, could I have a moment?" Bos asked.

"Do I know you?" Smith asked.

"No sir. I am from back east. I happened to read the article in the *Tribune* recently about you not wanting to sell or rent properties to Black people."

"Yes. Yes. A fine article. What did you think of my picture?"

"I thought it was great. I loved your picture. It was a great shot."

"So, what can I help you with, boy?"

"I'm concerned about your board not selling to Black people. We need homes just like everybody else. If we can afford to pay, why can't we live where we want to?"

"You seem like a well-spoken young man. You know that mixing of the races is not good. You see it all around. It's just not good. But I have an important luncheon I have to get to. Stop by my office, and we can talk further."

The offer sounded sincere. It was not.

Smith turned to his right and walked off. Bos thought that his original idea of figuring out a way to hurt this man was the best way to go.

"Well, that was successful. I guess we move onto the next plan. Take all his money," Nevin said.

"Looks that way. We know where he banks. He owns the bank. Are you ready for a stick up?"

Nevin smiled. "Nothing better than the smell of money in the morning."

The bank was only a block away. Smith had walked in the opposite direction. Nevin and Bos spent the day before surveying the bank. There was a steady flow of customers. At 2:00 p.m. the flow trailed off and there were very few people in the bank.

They entered through the front door. Two Black men with hats pulled down over their faces. The clerks in the bank were all white.

"We know where the safe is. Open it and give us everything and no one gets hurt."

The two robbers carried no firearms. Only axe handles. The safe was already open. Emptying the contents was easy. Nevin kept the lookout. There were two customers who were turned away. They were told the bank was having plumbing problems and would reopen in two hours. The customers accepted that in good form.

In less than 10 minutes, Bos had loaded the cash contents of the safe into two satchels.

The three female clerks and the male manager were led into the safe.

"Stay here for 10 minutes and you will be safe. If you come out before then, I can't guarantee your safety." Bos closed the safe door without locking it and then propped a high back chair against the armature on the outside of the safe door to prevent the occupants from easily opening the door. "Give Mr. M. L. Smith my regards," Bos said.

The Counterattack

Bos and Nevin exited the bank. Bos handed one satchel to Nevin and said, "See you at the train station. We can count the money on the way east."

Count it they did. Over $12,000 in cash. There were also 12 five-pound gold bars that had been wrapped in newspaper.

"What's he doing with gold bars?" Nevin asked.

"The Gold Standard. You can't go wrong with gold. Smart man. We need to let things calm down here. We'll come back to Chicago in about a month and give all this loot to the Binga State Bank. They have a fund set up to help Black families find housing."

The two brothers smiled at each other. *Good day's work*, they both thought.

Chapter Forty

Return to Monica
October 12, 1921
Harpers Ferry, West Virginia

"I know they're out there. I can hear 'em. I can smell 'em," Bos said.

"You can't smell 'em. You can't smell anything. You can't even smell your own stink," Nevin laughed.

"Yes I can. I know they're out there. Probably only one or two. We could go out and find 'em. Hunt 'em down. I'm not sure it's worth it. Let 'em watch. Let 'em make notes. Capone will come for us, but we'll be ready."

"Ready, Freddy. Nothing like it. Ready, Freddy. That's ol' Bos," Nevin laughed again.

"Guess who's comin'," Thomas asked as he walked up the drive toward the house.

"It's too early for Christmas," Bos said.

"It's Mr. Fancy himself. Must be trouble at the mine. Custer's burden. There's no end to the need for our services."

"Hello, Custers," Fancy Hart bellowed. "I bet you're all regretting the day you ever met me. I'm back again. I need your help," Fancy Hart said as he dismounted from the large draft horse that carried him. The horse breathed a sigh of relief when the 300-pound man got off his back.

"Trouble at the mine I bet," Bos said.

"They haven't honored a lick of that agreement that you wrote up, Bos. Not a lick."

The Counterattack

"I can't run the mine, Fancy. You men have to do that. What would you have me do?"

"We've been thinkin'. We could all run the mine. There's plenty of coal down there. It's not that deep. There's enough coal there to last our lifetimes. We'll buy them out. Run the mine. Support our families. That's our plan. Jacob thought you would like it. It leads to us being self-supportin'. But we need your fire power to convince the owners it's in their interest."

"I like your thinkin'. I like Jacob's thinkin'. I'll give you me and 10 of my men for one week. Do you think we can convince the owner in that time to sell?" Bos asked.

"I think that may do it. Leave in the mornin'?"

"You know my routine. Let's be on the road by 7:00 a.m."

Bos walked back into the house. He thought about the commitment he had just made. He needed to talk with Lee Ann. He knew that it would not be a happy conversation. He knew he had not been fair to her. Too much time away from home. The business was booming. The marriage was not. He needed to rethink his priorities and convince her that he meant it.

Chapter Forty-One

Miners' Melee
October 13, 1921
Lady Monica, West Virginia

Bos was familiar with the landscape. He knew that confronting the owner's roughnecks at the mine opening would result in unnecessary injury. Mostly to the miners and their families. He chose to take the battle to the owners. The owner's complex was on the other side of the mountain. Twelve miles away. Bos and Fancy Hart in one vehicle. Jacob Foster, Joe Williams, and Bos's 10 men were spread out among three other vehicles. Bos had come prepared. Lewis guns, hand grenades, and plenty of Thompsons.

There wasn't going to be a new agreement this time. Bos came as a lawgiver. The owner would follow the law he laid down.

They stopped one half mile outside of the owner's complex.

Bos spoke to the gathered men. "I want the Lewis guns up high. Three different emplacements. One at each end of the complex and one in the middle. They only come into play as a last resort. Our Thompsons and Springfields should get the job done. If not, the Lewis guns come into action."

"Bos, this road is a dead end. There's no way out except the way we came in," Jacob Foster said.

"That's good. Let's all get up on the high ground. Each man takes 4 hand grenades. We have belts that they fit into. Each of us will throw down two hand grenades. Throw 'em into open areas alongside structures but not into structures. That should bring the boys outside. Once I confirm there's nobody inside the main house, we torch it. Anyone

The Counterattack

who tries to put out the flame is fair game. Let's otherwise keep the killing to a minimum. That will be their call."

They climbed up about 50 feet above the complex. The Lewis gun emplacements were secured. Bos gave the signal for the hand grenades to be thrown: 20 plus hand grenades in quick succession.

The owner's complex consisted of 12 to 14 buildings. The one in the center was probably the home base of the boss. Sure enough, the boss came running into the street with the explosions rattling the small town. He stood in the middle of the street and looked up the hill behind his house. He took aim with a .45 handgun. Bos did not hesitate. He shouldered his Springfield and fired off two rounds. The first round blew out the man's knee. The second round hit the man's foot.

There were at least 25 other men who exited the multiple buildings. They were all heavily armed. There was no sense of any retreat on their part.

Bos gave the signal to open fire. "Fire only at those who are firin' back. Do not shoot into the buildings. We don't know who else is in there."

The order was clear. Bos ran from tree to tree to make sure the men were following his orders.

The company roughnecks were all skilled fighters. They took cover and took aim. Most of them only had handguns. The one man who had a Thompson was quickly identified. Bos focused on him with his Springfield. The first round entered his head.

Bos was fascinated that the boss man was still lying in the street in front of his home. No one had come to aid him. Mercenaries are like that. Loyal to the dollar but nothing else.

The firing subsided. Bos could see that the company men were dug in. They were dug in on the opposite side of the town street. The Lewis guns had achieved their effect. The company men knew that Bos and his men were well armed.

"The Lewis guns stay in place. The rest of us will split up. Half go to the right and come back down the town street. The rest of us will go to the left and will come up the town street. We can create a crossfire situation. We'll drive 'em further down the hillside or kill 'em. We are not takin' prisoners. We gave them fair warnin'. We gave 'em the chance to treat the miners fair. They chose not to."

The encircling motion took 15 minutes. Bos began firing from the downhill position, trying to clear the hillside on the opposite side of the town street. The total number of company men down there was between 12 and 15. The six men with him all had Thompsons. All but the miners were experienced with the weapon. The amount of lead it put out was incredible. One of the company men had a long-barrel rifle. An experienced rifle man. He knelt behind a single tree and picked off two of Bos's men. Bos shouldered his Springfield and fired one round at the large pine the man was hiding behind. The round hit the side of the tree to Bos's left. It took a large chunk out of the tree. Bos knew the man would pause and then look out from the other side of the tree. As his head emerged Bos fired. The man rolled down the hill not knowing what hit him.

The gunfire was now sporadic. Bos knew that the company men had either been killed or fled. The one who was left was the boss lying in the middle of the street.

"I thought we had a deal, Ebeneezer. You signed off on it. The miners tell me they kept their part of the deal. You did not. Why not?"

"We did. We kept the deal. Who's telling you we didn't?"

"I am," said Fancy Hart walking down the street. "I am. You're not paying us what was agreed to. You're overcharging us at the company store. You know what you're doing. You know darn well."

"I am judge, jury, and executioner, Ebeneezer. Tell me whether you kept the deal or not," Bos said.

"Okay. Okay, maybe Fancy is right. We cut some corners."

Bos walked toward the man, unholstered his .45, and shot the man in the head.

"Can you men run this mine? Can you men manage this mine and make a profit?"

"We can. The energy companies that buy coal don't care where it comes from. They want quality coal like this mine has. We can mine it, we can ship it, and we can get them to pay for it," Jacob Foster said.

"The mine is yours. It's yours to lose. I'll be here another week with my men to protect you. You better get things in order and get this place hummin'. Now we got some bodies to bury."

Chapter Forty-Two

The Company Store
October 14, 1921
Lady Monica, West Virginia

"Man, they had two stores. One store for us. One store for them. Can you believe that?" Fancy Hart said.

"I can believe it," Nevin said. "You see it all the time. Double standard. Pops calls it the triple standard. One standard for the rich folk. A different standard for the poor folk. Then a third standard for the Black folk. He said it's been around a long time. Long before our time. It ain't gonna change unless you change it. Do you want change? You make it happen."

"You're wise beyond your years. In addition, you're just copyin' what Pops says." Bos stepped into the stores. "Looks like the land of plenty. Here's what we're gonna do. Both stores are open. They'll be open from 7:00 a.m. to 12:00 noon. Folks who need groceries come and get 'em. You only take what you need. No charge."

"Who's going to be payin' for all this?" Nevin asked.

"The mine is. Make the mine profitable, and it can pay for your food. It can pay for a whole lot more. Fancy, you look like a man that could eat everything in the store. You better not. You only take what you need and maybe something less. Might help with your girth. Tomorrow, we start figurin' out how to run this business. The mine. The store. The men. We got a lot to do," Bos said.

"Pops would be proud of you. Helpin' the workingman. Helpin' the workingman support his family with an honest wage. You are a sight to behold," Nevin said.

The Counterattack

"Nope. Nothin' new about me. Nothin' new about what I do. We were taught by the master to respect where we came from. He came from nothin'. Whippings. Beatings. All day workin' in the field. No excuses. No time off. That's what he knew. He never forgot it. Never forgot where he came from and what he came with," Bos said.

Nevin stepped up on a ladder that was leaning against the store wall. "Some of you have met our father, Cookie Custer. George Armstrong Custer gave him the name Cookie. He took Custer from the general. The general paid the Black men who fought for him. He worked them hard. They fought hard from Gettysburg to Petersburg. General gave no quarter and expected none. That's what you men are gonna have to expect and receive from each other. If you want to make this work, it's gonna be your blood and sweat. Gettin' by is not an option. You excel or you fail. There is no in between. Are you ready?"

"We're ready." The gathered responded by clapping.

Bos walked around the store. He studied the inventory. The shelves were all fully stocked in both stores. The shelves in the other store were stocked with better quality, more of it, and lower prices.

That all changed today. It was not a company store. It was just a store for the people.

Chapter Forty-Three

Taking Care of Business
October 15, 1921
Lady Monica, West Virginia

"Bos, it won't work that way," Jacob Foster said.

"That's what people always say to me. It won't work. Don't tell me it won't work unless you can explain to me *why* it won't work," Bos replied.

"The good stuff, stuff that our buyers are willin' to pay top dollar for, is down deep. The only way you get there is by runnin' a shaft down vertically and then shafts horizontally out from the center of the hub."

"All that makes good sense. The risk here is the methane and collapse. You can't get the methane out of those horizontal shafts. You can shore 'em up with all the lumber you want, but they ain't gonna withstand a collapse."

Both men paused. They looked at each other. Bos smiled. "Here's what I'm proposin'. We dig a big hole down deep. We already got one. At the same time, we're diggin' both vertically and horizontally. The men who are diggin' horizontally are suspended on ropes secured at ground level. They cut away the coal, and it falls into a tarp underneath them. Once the tarp is close to being heavy enough, we have an electric motor that pulls the tarp up and empties it into a nearby rail car. The men on the bottom of the bed are digging down and loading their coal onto a smaller tarp at shoulder height. When the smaller tarp is filled, we hoist 'em up and empty 'em into a coal car. Diggin' down is hard work, but it reduces the chance of collapse. It lets the methane escape.

The men all wear helmets, goggles, shoulder pads, and masks over their faces. If they work protected, we can eliminate the safety issue. The coal may not be the same quality as what you get down deep, but it's coal. They'll be plenty of it. Make sense?"

"I like the idea," said Fancy Hart. "How is the hoist at the top going to work?"

"A tetrahedron. Three beams anchored at the side of the hole that meet in the center at an angle. The hoist will be suspended from these beams that are gonna have to be 75 to 100 feet long. We'll anchor all four in place at the same time so that they meet at the center of the hole. The hoist will be attached to that junction point. You've got a good stream over there, so we can generate electricity to power the winch to pull up the tarps. This can all work if you want it to. With this approach, you don't have to worry about the methane killin' you or blowin' up. If you have a collapse, then everything collapses into the center. Men diggin' horizontally will be able to get out. The men down at the bottom will have safety ropes to rappel up. In Northern France, more than once we had to go up into the mountains. We all became familiar with rock climbin' and rappellin'. We can teach you how to do it. Ain't foolproof. But it's better than what you got. Plus, I think you can produce a lot more coal."

The surrounding men nodded. They respected Bos. They knew he was smart. They knew he would help them. But they all said to themselves, "I'll believe it when I see it."

Chapter Forty-Four

Retribution
October 16, 1921
Lady Monica, West Virginia

"They're comin'," Bos said.

"Who?" asked Fancy Hart.

"The owners, the deputies and their goons."

"How do you know? I don't see anything."

"I've got watchers out there. Watchin'. Waitin'. And now reportin' back. There's over 100 of them. Well-armed and probably well-paid."

Bos began moving. He told the men to get the women and children down the hill and over into the holler. They would have some protection there. He sent one of his men with a Lewis gun to protect the women and children. He knew the owners' men would have no mercy. After the men were killed, all of the women and children would be killed.

"They're still about 5 miles away. They think they can troop 100 men through the woods and nobody will hear them. We'll set up inside the tree line. The two Lewis guns we'll set up at the highest point. We have plenty of ammo. Plenty of Thompsons. No time for target practice, but all of you miners need to understand the Thompson has a front hand grip for a reason. The muzzle pulls up. You need to keep it down and level with the front hand grip. Otherwise, all of your rounds go high."

Bos and his men handed out the Thompsons and entrenching tools. "We dig trenches along the tree line. That'll be your foxhole. Give it up and we're all dead. That includes your wives and children. You ain't

The Counterattack

fightin' for that mine. You're fightin' for your lives and your families. There'll be no retreat. If you got to fight them with the entrenching tools, you do so."

"Bos you gonna stay with us?" one of the miners asked.

"Nothin' I like better than a good fight. You men may not know it, but I have a family too. A wife, a little boy, and another one on the way. I'm fightin' for them too. They ain't here, but they're here in spirit. We'll see this through together or we will all die tryin'."

Bos had figured the attackers would spread out and come at the miners from several directions. Not so. They were marching in single file straight at the mine. Their arrogance was undiminished.

The miners dug a line of fox holes along the tree line. They knew how to dig. Fancy Hart had taken over the leadership of the miners. Jacob Foster was a good man. He had no stomach for killing. At 300 pounds, Hart had a stomach for anything.

An hour later, the troops could be heard in the distance. They were not accustomed to carrying a pack and rifle through the woods. Their fatigue showed itself in their movements.

The Lewis guns spoke first. The two emplacements were about 100 yards apart. The lead contingent of attackers advanced to within the range of the Lewis guns. The Lewis guns opened fire. The deputies, owners, agents, and goons didn't know what hit them. Some dove for cover behind nearby trees. The trees in the area were no more than 3 or 4 inches in diameter. They provided no cover. The .30-06 Springfield rounds penetrated many of the trees and the men behind them.

Bos gave the order for the miners on the tree line to open fire. The owners' men were now in a crossfire. Lewis guns fired from an uphill position. The miners firing head-on at the owners' men.

"Cease fire!" Bos called out.

Bos approached the line of fallen men. He could see some running away in the distance. He would not pursue. He looked back at the miners and shouted out, "We're takin' no prisoners. They would've had no mercy on you or your families. We'll show them none. Every man gets a bullet in the head. Any who can't stomach that can walk back to the mine. Nothin' will be held against you."

Bos took the lead. Most of the men on the ground were already dead. He put his Thompson on single fire and proceeded from body to body. He had proposed terms to the owners. The miners would run the mine and share the profits with the owners. The owners didn't have to do anything. Just count their earnings. That wasn't good enough. They'd come back again with a bigger force. Bos would train the miners how to be ready. He would give them the weapons to be ready.

Chapter Forty-Five

Firing Up
October 18, 1921
Lady Monica, West Virginia

"How do you heat your homes?" Bos asked.

"They gave us woodstoves. They don't look like much, but they do spread the heat," Fancy Hart said.

"You need to come into the 20th century. I saw electric lights over in the owners' compound. Where are they gettin' the electricity?"

"The nearby river. They dammed up part of it. They control the flow. There are two paddle wheels down below the dam. They get the electricity. We use handheld lamps in the mine and manpower to push the carts. That's only fair," Fancy said.

"Never mind about fair. Life ain't supposed to be fair. Life is what you make it. We can use those paddle wheels to create generators to power our diggin' devices, hoists, and your homes. Do you understand how a generator works?"

"Nope. It sounds like I'm gonna learn."

"Fancy, you need to understand how things work in order to make 'em work. You got two paddle wheels on the river. Those paddle wheels can mechanically turn the spinnin' coil of wire in the generator. The coil is between two magnets that convert the mechanical energy of the spinnin' coil into electric energy. With that we can power electric lights for your homes and also power diggin' and haulin' devices to get the coal out of the ground. Do you know the coal buyers?" Bos asked Fancy.

"I met them a year ago. They work for a power company in Virginia. They like our coal because it's rich. They'll take any coal we can deliver. The north-south rail line is only a mile from here. It's used only for coal transport."

"How do you get the coal to the rail line?"

"The owners sent trucks once a week. They haul it to the rail line."

"Those truckers are local. They'll work for whoever pays. You need to find 'em and get 'em on schedule to haul at least as much coal as they have in the past."

"I can do that. Can I borrow your car to go into town?"

"You know how to crank it?"

"Yep."

"Tell Foster and Williams I need to see 'em. We need to get goin' on diggin' this coal out of the surface. Your men need to understand the workday starts at 6:00 a.m. and ends at 6:00 p.m. They can walk home for lunch."

Bos knew that he had a lot to learn about mining. Surface mining was not the same as going deep. He understood that. Going deep was not workable. What he knew is that he could go deep enough to get good coal and get it in greater quantity faster. What he hadn't told Fancy Hart and the others was that the road to success meant that these miners, at least for some time, would have to work 12-hour days seven days a week.

He figured they might grumble. He needed to talk to the wives. They would understand his mining technique was safer. Resulted in fewer accidents. In the long run, it would produce more coal and better coal for more money. They understood money. Simple as they might be, everybody seemed to understand that.

Chapter Forty-Six

Rearming
October 21, 1921
Lady Monica, West Virginia

Bos had looked at the landscape. There were two ways in. He would stagger the four Lewis guns along those two routes. They would be positioned so that each gunner could fall back and leave the gunner on the other side of the roadway still in fixed position and with good coverage of the roadway.

The women would have to help out with the mine security. He figured they could work in four-hour shifts. They would trek out in the four compass directions. One half hour out and one-half hour back. Any who didn't return would signal trouble.

"First thing we do is build a schoolhouse. The children need schoolin'. I need a volunteer to be the teacher," Bos said.

No hands rose from the assembled crowd of families.

"Either volunteer, or I pick a volunteer."

Bos motioned to Fancy Hart. "Who is the smartest among 'em?"

"No question. It's my wife."

"I haven't met her. Don't tell me her name is Fanny."

"Bos Custer, you're the second smartest man I've ever met."

"I don't want to meet the smartest."

"He's gone. He was my pappy. Not much schooling, but he knew how to read. Self-taught. He knew how to count change. He knew how to stand his ground. You remind me of him. Except you're a little fella compared to him. He was bigger than I am."

"We start the schoolhouse tomorrow. We'll build it to the west on the opposite ridge. It'll be a five-minute walk. That will put some distance between the children and the minin'. Maybe give 'em some incentive to not become miners."

Bos talked with his two brothers. "Nevin, you need to set up a target range. All of these men and women need to learn how to use the Lewis guns, Winchesters, and Springfields that we brought. Once we get the schoolhouse built, we'll have target practice every morning at 9 :00 a.m. People can rotate attendance so that everybody practices once a week. You and Thomas can take charge of that for the next week. You need to also teach the women how to walk through the woods while makin' no noise and spottin' any intruders. Good surveillance and good protection are gonna be the key to this mine survivin'. No slackers. Everybody contributes or they all fail together."

"These are hard-workin' people, Bos. But they're simple people. They like to do things their own way," Fancy said.

"That's fine. Right now they're fightin' for survival. You need to convince 'em they fight together, they stand together, they lock arms together, or they all die. Simple as that. When the owners come back, and they will, they'll be comin' back to kill each and every one of you and to take this hole in the ground back. Make sure they understand that. If anyone wants out, tell 'em to leave now. I don't know these people. You do. You say they're simple people. I'm a simple man. Lay down simple rules, and make sure they follow them. Got it?"

"Got it."

Chapter Forty-Seven

Diggin'
October 24, 1921
Lady Monica, West Virginia

The vertical mineshaft went down 150 feet. Bos had measured it with rope. The elevator up and down was just a manlift. One man was pulled up at a time with two men at the top pulling and pushing on the rope elevator that brought the ascending miner up. The process had been easier when they worked in shifts. One miner up and one miner down at the same time. The miners had complained to the owner about the shift work because it meant each shift spent several hours without the benefit of any daylight. They felt it affected productivity and safety. The owners relented.

Bos had envisioned several dig sites. Each dig site would be overshadowed with a tetrahedron structure that supported the tarp, which would collect the dirt and coal to be offloaded. The shaft downward would be 20 feet by 20 feet. As they hit good coal, the size of the shaft would be expanded. The tarps would be hauled up and unloaded. The dirt would be spread around the perimeter of the mining area to serve as a protective shield when the owners returned. It was hard work. The miners were showing they were up to it. Bos and his brothers appreciated that.

"I know you've been relyin' on Fancy. I'm okay with that. He's got a better head on those big shoulders than I do. I've spent too many years in the mines to be quick-witted. I just want you to know, Bos, I don't hold that against you," Jacob Foster said.

"I appreciate that, Jacob. You're a good man. Part of the reason you're a good man is because you know your limits. So many I've met didn't. And didn't want to be told what those limits were," Bos said.

"I learned my limits in Northern France. Just like you did. I didn't know what it meant to keep my head down. I learned the first time a bullet sailed by my ear. You see this right ear. The part that's missing. A German bullet. Meant for my head but it just took a part of my ear. I started learning real quick. You learned or you died."

"You fought with the French?"

"Didn't we all. Our French commander didn't believe in kitchen patrol. Everyone rotated on the front lines. Nobody stayed back. Even the supply guys all knew they would see a fair share of frontline duty. Made a lot of sense. The French treated us well. Fed us well. And respected what we had to offer. We had some tough guys in our unit. Experienced killers. The Germans learned to fear us. The French learned quickly how to use our guys. We always fought alongside the French. They'd have two of our crazies lead the charge, and the French troops would follow. The commanders loved that."

"You were lucky."

"No. You were lucky. We heard all about the three of you. You were legend. You made all of us proud. We all felt we had to live up to what you had done."

"That means a lot to me, Jacob. You can teach these men a lot about fightin'. Most of them don't know that. All they know is backbreakin' work. Fightin' and stayin' alive means more than just sloggin' ahead. You gotta know where you're goin'."

Chapter Forty-Eight

Checkin' the Defense
October 25, 1921
Lady Monica, West Virginia

"You ladies are the heart of the security for this whole community. If you fail, the community fails. You need to understand the importance of what you're doin'. You need to walk without makin' noise. You need to see what's there to be seen. And you need to see what may not be there to be seen," Bos said.

"You going to show us how to do this?" one of the women asked.

"That's why I'm here. Let's talk about walkin'. You gotta walk on your toes. No flat feet. Before your foot goes down, you know what's there to step on. No twigs. No soft ground. If you don't know where to step, then stop. Look around. See who might be out there. It may be they don't have your trainin'. They may be comin' straight at you makin' noise. You gotta hear 'em."

"You know we're simple. But we ain't stupid. Show us what you mean."

Bos walked around them in a circle. After a minute, he told them to close their eyes. "In a minute I will tell you to open your eyes. Before you do that, I want you to point to where I am."

Bos hadn't worn his tracking shoes. The boots he had on would have to do. He began moving. In a minute, they opened their eyes. Only one of them pointed in the right direction.

"Was that a lucky guess, or did you know where I was?"

"My eyesight ain't real good. My sense of hearing is real good. You were quiet. I could hear you still," the woman said.

"That's good. You get the first shift. You know how to listen. You know how to interpret. That's what we need. You women are our ears. Without you, the enemy is upon us. You are our scouts. Each of you will be movin' in a compass direction. Thirty minutes out and thirty minutes back. If anyone doesn't come back on time, then you know we got a problem. That doesn't mean soundin' the full alarm. It does mean wakin' up some of the men and gettin' 'em ready. It may mean the attack is comin'."

"We got to do this at night also?" one of the women asked.

"Twenty-four hours a day, seven days a week. No rest. Four-hour shifts. Five women per shift. One person stays here at the hub. The other four are the spokes of the wheel. Can you do this?"

"You bet we can. The men work hard all day. We work hard also. We just need to get used to workin' a bit harder," the leader of the group said.

"I like your men. I like you too," Bos smiled as he approached each woman and shook her hand.

"I don't know what my husband will say when he hears I hugged another man. But I don't care," the leader said as she walked toward Bos. He smiled and hugged her too.

Chapter Forty-Nine

Dry Run
October 27, 1921
Lady Monica, West Virginia

Bos walked the mine area with Nevin and Thomas. The hole in the ground was now an excavation the size of a football field. At the center was a hole that was 20 by 20. The operation ran 12 hours a day. The amount of dirt and coal that was being hauled out created a mound around the excavation that was over 20 feet high. Four men spent full time just separating the dirt from the coal. The amount of coal being brought out of the mine was increasing daily. The coal being brought out today was dark and hard. The hole in the ground was more than 100 feet deep. Fancy Hart knew where the rich coal was, and the men were finding it.

The women were maintaining the watch. On the set schedule, the four spokes of the wheel returned to the hub, consumed some coffee, and then headed back out. They knew their role. They filled it.

"Let's take a ride," Bos said.

"Check on the Lewis guns?" Nevin asked.

"Yep. That's their first and best line of defense. If that fails, then the rest may fail. Fancy Hart is some organizer. He has all these people workin' together. They don't all get along but in spite of that, things work. He's made a new arrangement with the coal buyer. Startin' next Monday, the coal is picked up daily. He's made arrangement with a trucker to have six trucks here at 8:00 a.m. every morning. The train comes at noontime. He figures he can give them six good truckloads of black coal every day. He says there's been a lot of whinin' about the security, but the people understand it has to be. We'll find out tonight how good it is."

"What do you mean?" Thomas asked.

"Tonight we do a dry run. Tonight we're the owners' goons and we attack. We'll see how good the defense is."

At 10:00 that night, Bos and Nevin set out. Thomas was told he had the night off. Together they walked through the woods to a point about a mile outside of the mine. They timed their departure from the mine area with the time when all four spokes of the wheel would be returning to the hub. Once they'd gotten to a point about a mile from the hub, they proceeded to walk back toward the hub. Breaking twigs as they walked. Creating noises that were subtle but recognizable. The woman responsible for the western spoke was good. She heard the noises. She stopped on the track and listened. Bos had the sense that she knew that these noises were not the noises of someone trudging through the woods. She backtracked to the hub and reported what she had found. The woman in charge of the hub picked up her shotgun and proceeded on the western spoke. Bos could hear her coming. He could see the reflection of the shotgun from the moonlight.

He stood up and took cover behind a tree. "It's me, Bos Custer. I was checkin' your defense. You're good. You're damn good."

"You're almost dead, Mr. Custer. In fact, you may still be dead if you don't come out right away with your hands over your head."

Bos complied.

The woman approached. "You are Bos Custer. Only a crazy man would do what you did. I know you were just testing us. I guess we passed."

"With flyin' colors." They smiled at each other. They walked back to the hub arm and arm.

"Your shotgun. You need to do somethin' to reduce the glint. In the moonlight I could see reflections off it. That will give away your position. The bore needs to be oiled. The outside barrel will rust over time. Oiling it creates a reflection. You need to put some dirt on it. No reflections."

Chapter Fifty

Makin' Bacon
October 28, 1921
Lady Monica, West Virginia

The smell of pork was everywhere. It pierced the air. As the sun rose, the front doors of the houses opened. A sweet smell. They all recognized it. Some smiled. Some shook their heads. They knew who was at work. He'd been up since 4:00 a.m. Killed and cut the hog by 5:00 a.m. The large pit fire was flaming. The grease was dripping down. Bos kept the animal at least a foot above the flames. They never touched the meat. The secret was intense heat but no burning.

Fancy Hart was the first one to amble out. "Smells great, my friend. How long you been up?"

"I got up at my usual hour. Three-thirty. I think I've done what I can here. We'll be leavin' today. I wanted to cook all of you a good breakfast. Good way to start the day. Also a good way to say goodbye. I'll be nearby, but you folks need to make it on your own. I think you have a good defensive system when the owners come back. You've got 20 full-grown hogs. That's a start. You need to kill 'em sparingly. You kill the males first and then the females. You need to keep them in the pen. They taste great, but they are filthy and they need to be away from the community. The big cats will come huntin' for them. The 10-foot-high fence we've built may be enough. Don't assume the cats can't tear it down or get over it. They're crafty. Set up a string perimeter with bells on it about 20 yards out from the fence. That'll tell you when the cats are comin'. You need to have one marksman on call to come out and shoot the cats, otherwise your hogs won't last more than a few

The Counterattack

days. When you kill 'em, you need to drag 'em about a mile out into the woods. Hang 'em from a limb. The other animals will be on 'em in no time."

"Man, you're full of advice this morning. Is there any wisdom you got left?"

"A whole lot. But you've got the basics. As long as the coal is there to be dug, you folks can have a decent life here. Don't let your guard down. Don't forget the owners will be back. With a vengeance. You need to teach them another lesson."

"If we need help, can I call on you?"

"Anytime. One of my men came in late last night. We've got an intruder in Harpers Ferry. One of Capone's men. He's livin' in the bunkhouse. Don't know who he is. But he's killed one of our best men. Jack Johnson has been with me from the beginnin'. Fought in Northern France. A good man. He was killed in his sleep night before last. I know it's Capone's work. I need to get back to find the killer and hang him. When I do, I'll send his body to Capone."

"I'd hate to be your enemy, Bos Custer. You are a kind man. But I need to make sure I never cross you."

"You couldn't cross me. You don't have any guile. It takes guile to cross me. You are one of those people who was born without it. Not a lick of it. What you see is what you get with you. I like what I see. And I'm gonna miss you, Fancy Hart."

"Feeling's mutual."

"It may not be when I come callin'. And I will come callin'. The counterattack is in motion. I'm going to need some of your men and maybe some of the women too."

Chapter Fifty-One

The Players
October 29, 1921
Harpers Ferry, West Virginia

Jack Jackson had been with Bos from the beginning. A good man. He knew how to use a rifle. He was a skilled woodworker. He had built the barracks almost by himself. Each morning he had gone into the woods and identified the trees to be cut. He had them hauled back to the site where they were cut into two-by-fours, two-by-eights, or four-by-fours. His choice of wood had not always been consistent with Bos's thoughts, but the barracks he built were sturdy and provided good cover and protection for the men.

Jackson had been killed in his sleep. Throat slit. He had a room of his own in the barracks. It wasn't easy for someone to slip in and kill him.

The way Bos had set up the rotation of men was that they worked for 30 days and then had 30 days off with full pay. When they returned after their time off, they were expected to bring at least one new worker with them. The workforce was constantly changing. Many of the men never returned after their month off with pay. The work was hard. Bos was demanding. And he was unforgiving. Bos tried to interview all of the new men. With a workforce of over 50, he had trouble keeping track of them all. The men were all Black. Bos had not cared what color they were. He knew he would only be able to attract Black men. He didn't care. He just wanted men who wanted to work hard, long hours and not complain. For the most part, he had gotten that. There were three whom he had identified as being potential problems. Jasper Crittenden had

The Counterattack

been caught stealing from some of the other men. Beaufort Cunningham was a loner. He kept to himself and didn't say a word. If his work had been exemplary, he wouldn't have been noticed by Bos. It was not. Bojangles Robinson said he was related to the dancer. He might've been. Bos didn't care. He provided entertainment for the men.

He would focus on these three. They were newcomers. They were the type that Capone might've been able to buy. All three had a type of ruthlessness about them that Bos identified with. They were killers. Just like him.

"I'll be sleepin' in the barracks for the next few nights. Nevin, I want you on patrol from 9:00 p.m. to 5:00 a.m. I know your wife may not care for that. This is not gonna be the last of the murders. This man was hired by Capone. He is paid by Capone. He will murder for Capone. We need to stop him, otherwise we lose all of our workers," Bos said.

"How come I always get the shit jobs?" Nevin asked.

"You don't. The job I'm givin' Thomas is even worse. He's gonna be the decoy. He's gonna sleep in Hiram Walker's room and wait for the killer to come after him. Hiram will sleep in the house."

"How come we never get any say in these decisions?" Thomas asked.

"It's called chain of command. You know how it works. There has to be somebody in charge. We're not a democracy here. I don't ask you to do anything I wouldn't do," Bos replied.

They all knew that was so.

Chapter Fifty-Two

Hang 'em High
October 31, 1921
Harpers Ferry, West Virginia

Hiram Walker was six feet tall. He weighed 220 pounds. A big man. He walked on the balls of his feet and was ready to sprint into action if he ever had to. He had grown up in the city of Washington, DC. He loved the city. The duplex house that his family lived in was on Southern Avenue. Southern Avenue separated Washington, DC, from Prince Georges County, Maryland. He lived right near Marlboro Pike.

When he joined the US Army in 1917, he was 17 years old. He thought it would be an adventure. It was. Just not the type he thought of. He was quickly labeled an octoroon. He had at least 1/8 Black blood in him. That made him a Black man. He was very light complected. Could pass as a white man in most circumstances. He had never tried to pass. He was happy being a Black man. He had had some white acquaintances. They weren't friends, but they got along. The US Army changed that. He was a Black man, according to the US Army. He would never be anything else again.

Basic training had been an experience. He was put into a white platoon. When it was discovered he was an octoroon, he was moved to the Black platoon. He didn't care. He didn't care if they called him Black or white or something in between. He had joined for the adventure. That's the only thing he wanted. Just adventure. Everything else was water off his back.

He trudged through the forest on the south end of the Custer property. He knew there was a deer crossing there. Armed with his

The Counterattack

Winchester, he knew that if he positioned himself well, he could bag one deer and drag it back to the camp. It would provide good meat for many meals. What he hadn't expected was that somebody would be shooting at him.

It was a .22 round. It penetrated the bill of his hat. Not fired by a marksman. A .22 rifle was easy to handle. No kick. No vibrations. Just point-and-shoot. The shooter could point. But he couldn't shoot.

Walker took cover. Was it a stray shot? Or was it intended for him? He didn't know. He knew in Northern France there were no such thing as stray shots. They were all intended for a target. He assumed that was the case here. From the impact of the round, he concluded that the shooter was to the west. Walker positioned himself to provide maximum protection. He kept his Winchester close to his body. He knew there would be a second round to follow. The large oak he was hiding behind was his friend. It absorbed the next round and gave him the line of sight to the shooter.

Walker could see the rustling of bushes in the distance. The shooter was 200 feet away. He was moving to the north. Away from Walker. No sense in wasting time. He moved in a due north direction as was the shooter.

Walker figured the shooter was probably a city boy. Not used to rifles. He picked the .22 because it was accurate and had no kick. He figured he would wound Walker and then move in for the kill. The wounding had been the problem. Now he was on the run. And being chased by an experienced hunter.

Walker moved through the forest without effort. He knew how to position his feet so as to minimize noise. He carried his rifle at port arms with a round chambered. If he had a shot, he would take it standing up.

Walker was within 50 feet of the shooter when he saw it. The ground had been disturbed. There had been an attempt to disguise it, but a poor attempt. He slowed as he approached the disturbed earth. He picked up a rock that weighed no more than five pounds and threw it at the disturbed area. The covering gave way. The rock fell into a hole that was four feet deep. He drew in closer behind the oak tree that was protecting him. He had to reassess this shooter. He was not just a city boy. He had cunning. He had experience. He knew how to draw his prey in. He knew how to trap him.

Walker decided this man probably was his match. He had to assume that. Otherwise he'd be dead very soon. He decided the head-on approach was not the right way. He would track him. But track him from the rear to avoid any future traps.

The shooter was on the move again. Walker moved 50 feet to the west and then headed north to keep track of the shooter. The man had endurance. Walker was an experienced runner and tracker. He could go for hours. The shooter was now moving at a good pace. It was a pace that told Walker this man knew where he was going and knew how to get there.

What Walker didn't know was that he was being tracked.

When Walker got within 50 feet of the shooter, he stopped, leaned against a tree, and fired off his first round. It hit the shooter in the back. Walker could see the heavy pack that the man had been carrying. The man and the pack fell to the ground.

The next sound was from the round that entered the back of Walker's head. No doubt a Springfield round.

The first shooter circled back. The large pack on his back had saved him from Walker's shot. Within the pack he had a large E-Tool. It was made of heavy steel. Probably too heavy to be useful as an entrenching tool. But heavy enough to stop or deflect a Winchester round.

The Counterattack

They looked at each other. They nodded.

"String him up?" the first shooter said.

"That's what Capone ordered," the second man said.

He looped a rope over a branch that was 20 feet above. Tied the rope around Hiram Walker's neck and pulled him up and secured the rope.

The deed was done. They would keep killing until they were caught or until Capone attacked.

Chapter Fifty-Three

Interrogation
November 1, 1921
Harpers Ferry, West Virginia

"We need to talk," Bos said to Beaufort Cunningham.

"About what, Bos?" Cunningham asked.

"About things in general. I'd like to get to know you better."

"When?"

"How about you come up to the house now. I can give you some of my wife's lemonade, and we can talk."

"I'll be up right soon," Cunningham responded.

Lee Ann was concerned about what was happening. The men were anxious. They didn't mind fighting an enemy they could see. They didn't like not being able to see the enemy.

She and Bos had agreed that they would interview the men one by one. There were three of them that Bos had focused on. Lee Ann had little contact with the men. She didn't know who the suspects could be. The interviews would take place in the main house. Bos would do the questioning. Lee Ann would do the listening. Either in the same room where the questioning was done or in an adjoining room where she could eavesdrop.

Bos knew his wife had a better sense of human nature than he did. He relied on that. She did have to remind him from time to time.

Cunningham knocked on the front door. Compared to the Custer men, he was small. Five feet eight. Maybe 140 pounds soaking wet. He had a big smile on his face. "Afternoon, Mrs. Custer. Bos asked me to stop up."

The Counterattack

"Of course. Come in. Can I get you some lemonade?" Lee Ann asked.

"That'd be nice. Thank you, ma'am."

"So where you from?"

"Born in North Carolina. Came north about 15 years ago with my family. Lived in DC most of my life."

"My father-in-law has a place in DC. Have you met Cookie?"

"I have not. I heard about him. Understand he's a big man. I mean a really big man."

"He is that. So what school you go to in DC?"

"We ain't had no time for school. Too busy workin'. Tryin' to put food on the table. I was 15 when I came north. Started workin' right away. Worked down on the train yard on Florida Avenue. Loadin' and unloadin'. Hard work but it did pay. My daddy ran off with some other woman two years after we came north. So it was just my mom and two brothers. We did OK. One of my brothers was killed in the war. When I tried to volunteer, Mama said no. She wasn't about to lose two sons. I thought about goin' anyhow but nobody could tell me what the war was all about. So I figured why go to war if you don't know what you're fightin' for. Made no sense to me."

"Where is your other brother?"

"He's a conductor. Works on the trains. Gone back and forth across the country many times. Says he loves it. I believe him. He actually lives on the trains. When they're in station, he sleeps in one of the rooms. Can't imagine that. I like havin' a home. Even if it is just a bunkhouse like what we got here."

"How long you think you'll be stayin' with us?"

"I haven't decided yet. I like it here. I like outdoor work. I like hard work. I also like the pay. Thirty days on. Thirty days off with full pay.

Can't beat that. I'm surprised there's not a steady stream of men comin' out this way for work."

"We are too. How did you hear about us?"

"My brother, the conductor. He says there's a lot of people talkin' about you. How you makin' liquor. How you sellin' it to Black churches. How those Black churches able to do it and make money off the liquor. I figured you must be doing somethin' right. Either you got God on your side, or you got the devil on your side."

"So, which is it?"

"No question. No question at all. You got them both on your side. The pastors and the pushers, as they say. The pastors are blessing the alcohol, and the pushers are movin' it."

Bos could hear all of this from the kitchen. He smiled when he heard Cunningham describe him as a pusher.

"I appreciate you comin' up, Cunningham. I see you're enjoying my wife's lemonade. A bit too sweet for me. But I still drink it," Bos said as he entered the room.

"You are a lucky man, Mr. Custer."

"I am indeed. Tommy tells me you've been gettin' pretty good with the .22. That's okay for squirrel huntin'. We don't do much of that out here. Probably need to start workin' more on the Springfield and the Winchester. Has Tommy given you any lessons on the Lewis gun?"

"I'll be in the kitchen if you need me," Lee Ann said. When she entered the kitchen, she stood by the door. She could hear the entire conversation.

Bos continued talking with Cunningham about his daily routine. "Why the .22? Most men who haven't grown up around guns move straight to the Winchester."

"It's light. I like the feel of it. I'm not that big of a man. A Springfield or Winchester is built more for a bigger man. A man like you."

"We were lookin' for you yesterday afternoon. Nobody knew where you were. You need to keep Tommy Johnson informed of where you are. If you want to go down to the range to shoot, you can do that. Just keep him posted."

"Yesterday afternoon? I was in the bunkhouse. I drank some of that cider. I don't know who made it. I don't know how long it had been in the bunkhouse. It was bad. It did somethin' to my stomach. I'll make up for the time I lost. You know I work hard," Cunningham said.

"I know you do. How are you feelin' now?"

"Much better. Much better."

Bos continued talking with Cunningham for another 30 minutes. They talked about the job. How he was fitting in. What his plans were.

As they were finishing, Lee Ann came back into the dining room.

"I enjoyed talkin' with you. Can I call you Beau? I understand that's what you go by," Bos asked.

"That's what everybody calls me."

"Oh, one other thing. Could I take a look at your .22? I heard that model of .22 had some trouble with the bolt action," Bos asked.

"I'll go down to the bunkhouse and get it," Cunningham offered.

"Let's go down together and take a look. I'll be back in a few," Bos said to Lee Ann.

They walked side-by-side out of the house and down toward the bunkhouse.

"When was the last time you fired the .22?" Bos asked Cunningham.

"It's been a couple of weeks. You keep us so busy we don't have time for target practice."

"That's not my goal. If you need more time at the range, tell me. I'm happy to take you down there and give you some pointers. We need men who know weapons and know how to use 'em. That's important."

They entered the bunkhouse and Cunningham turned to the right to where his bunk was. He picked up the .22 and handed it to Bos.

"Who was your range master when you first fired this at the range?" Bos asked.

"I think it was Hiram."

"I know he taught you weapons protocol. When you hand a weapon to anyone, you clear the action and make sure the weapon is either breached or the action is open. You did neither. Why not?"

"You're right. Hiram did teach us that. I just forgot."

Bos looked at the man as he spoke. Bos looked down at the .22. With the action open, he looked down the barrel from the muzzle end. The weapon had not been cleaned in some time. He looked down the barrel from the other end and could see a buildup of powder. The powder inside the chamber was of recent origin. It had not been there two weeks.

"Thanks, Cunningham. This weapon needs to be cleaned. I appreciate you talkin' with me."

Bos walked back to his home. He knew the bullet hole through the bill of Walker's hat came from a .22.

Chapter Fifty-Four

Bojangles
November 1, 1921
Harpers Ferry, West Virginia

Bos knew about Bojangles Robinson. The real one. He was born in Richmond, Virginia. His given name was Luther. He went by Bill. Bos knew him as a rifleman in Northern France. He wasn't dancing then. After the war, he became famous in the clubs in New York for his freestyle dancing.

"So, you're related to Robinson?" Bos asked.

"Yep. He was my daddy's brother. My uncle. Same last name. My first name is James. I like dancing. This would be a fun house for dancing. Hardwood floors. High ceilings. Lots of open space. I could put on a show here." Robinson said.

"Well let's see it. Help me pull the table over toward the back," Bos said to Robinson.

Together they moved the large table to the back of the open room. Cleared away all the chairs.

"It's all yours, Mr. Robinson."

Robinson was wearing work boots. Not exactly tap shoes. It didn't slow him down. He was a whirling dervish. His swinging graceful movements were a thing to behold. Lee Ann came in the room. She smiled as Robinson danced. Put her arms around her husband and together they swayed with the beat Robinson created through his feet.

"I could go on forever if you let me," Robinson said.

"How come a dancer like you is out here in the woods?" Lee Ann asked.

"This dancer likes the woods. Likes the outdoors. Likes the freedom." Robinson finished his show with a quick flurry of taps on the floor. He took a bow.

"So, tell me what you know about your dancin' uncle," Bos asked.

"Not that much. He was born in Richmond. Served in the war. I didn't see that much of him. I was told he led the parade after the war in New York City. I grew up in North Carolina. Had no real contact with him, but my father did. He came down to visit once or twice. Gave us all dance lessons, which we never forgot. So here I am in West Virginia making alcohol and dancing for my boss."

"I was lookin' for you yesterday afternoon. Couldn't find you," Bos said.

"I was down by the range. It looked like you needed more swinging targets, so I put them up. Cut up the wood and made the posts for the swinging pieces. Took about three hours. Let me know what you think."

"Sounds like good work. Let's go down and take a look at it."

Bos said goodbye to his wife. Bojangles nodded to her.

They walked together in silence toward the range.

"Where did you learn to shoot the Winchester?" Bos asked.

"In North Carolina. It wasn't easy for a Black man to own a rifle. A lot of stores wouldn't sell them. Afraid we'd use them on the white folk. My daddy bought me one before he left. I fired it almost daily. Wasn't easy paying for the ammo. Most of the time I just stole it. Down there people would leave it laying around. A box of shells was expensive. But if I found one laying around it was mine."

"Can you hit that far stationary target at 100 yards?"

"Easy. Easy Peezy. If I had my Winchester here, I'd show you. I know you can do that. I've heard about you."

The Counterattack

"I'll take you up on that. Let's walk back. I got a few more things to do before dinner time. I appreciate you comin' down," Bos said.

They walked back in silence to the house. Robinson nodded and walked toward the barracks. Bos headed into the house.

"Well tell me about it." Lee Ann asked.

"There's not much to tell. But neither of these guys can account for where they were at important times. He sounds believable. I like his dancin'. But I don't like him."

"Why not?" his wife asked.

"Women's intuition. Call it what you will. I don't like him. There's somethin' wrong. During the war, Bojangles Robinson put on a show for the Black troops. We were about 50 miles north of Paris. Robinson had built his own dance floor. He danced on it. For about an hour. Afterward I talked with him. I didn't just talk, we drank. A lot. We talked about family, about our homes. We talked about the stupid war. We talked about everything. He never mentioned a brother, and he never mentioned a brother with children. I think he would've if they existed."

Chapter Fifty-Five

Tommy
November 2, 1921
Harpers Ferry, West Virginia

"I think they're comin' for you," Bos said.

"Who?" Tommy Johnson asked.

"Capone's men. They're here. They've already killed two of us. I think they're gunnin' for you."

"I appreciate the honor. I know who you're talking about. I've been suspicious of their movements. The three of them seem to have something going. They think we don't notice. I do. I suggest we take 'em out in the woods and string 'em up. I bet they tell us the truth."

"I want to talk with Jasper first. I think he might be the soft spot. After I talk with him, then we lay the trap. That is if you're willin'."

"I'm willing for anything. Especially if it saves my neck. What do you have in mind?"

"Probably a little hike in the woods. These guys seem to act in duos. But it could be all three of 'em each time. I don't know for sure. But we need to be prepared to outgun 'em. My brothers and I and you make four. We need to lure 'em into the woods to see what they do. Once they start following the scent, then we know we got our bad actors."

"Okay. When do we start?"

"I'm talkin' with Jasper this morning. Get the word out that you're doin' some deer huntin' this afternoon. I'll have Thomas and Nevin in place by 12 noon."

Bos shook hands with Johnson and walked down to the bunkhouse.

The Counterattack

Jasper Crickenden was sitting on his bed. He was cleaning his Winchester rifle. The weapon shined. The long cleaning rod was being run up and down the bore.

"The other men tell me you clean that rifle every day. Do you shoot it every day?" Bos asked.

"I try to. Practice does make perfect. I know I'll never get there, but I'm tryin'." Crickenden said.

"I like that attitude," Bos said. "Would you mind comin' up to the house so we can have a chat. You've been doin' a lot of good work, and I'd like to get to know you a little better."

"When?"

"No time like the present."

Crickenden finished up cleaning his weapon. He put the cleaning instruments away and hung the Winchester on the wall over his bed. "I'm ready when you are."

The two men walked out of the bunkhouse. Bos had already arranged with his wife that she would be present. He wanted her input on these men—what she thought they were made of, and what kind of men they were.

"Good mornin' glory," Bos hollered as he entered the house.

"Good mornin' sunshine," the female voice replied.

Crickenden smiled. He had seen Lee Ann Custer around the complex. He had never gotten close to her. She was a beauty. Long flaxen hair. Trim figure. Always had a bright smile on her face. She entered the dining room area with a smile leading the way.

Crickenden returned the smile. "Good mornin', ma'am. I'm Jasper Crickenden."

"I know. Bos pointed you out to me not too long ago," Lee Ann replied. "He said you were a fine marksman. Bos appreciates that."

"Thank you, Mrs. Custer."

"Have a seat," Bos said. "You probably heard we had Robinson come visitin' the other day. He gave us a dance show. Pretty entertainin'. You dance?"

"No sir. I'm just a shooter. Love that Winchester. Used to have one of my own, but a white man stole it from me. Said I couldn't be trusted with one. I felt like shootin' him, but I didn't."

"Smart decision. You fought?"

"I wanted to. When they were lookin' for volunteers, I was only 17. I'm 21 now. I wanted to fight, but they wouldn't take me. I should've just forged my mama's signature to the papers. She wouldn't have liked that. She brought me up to be honest. So I was. So no, I did not fight. But I grew up in the woods of North Carolina. I can shoot a deer at 200 yards and hit 'em right in the heart. I don't believe in those automatic weapons. That's not shootin'. That's just a sprayin'. Anyone can do that."

"I like that attitude. Sometimes we don't have the luxury of using a Winchester. Sometimes we need to rely on the repeaters. You fired a Thompson?"

"Oh yeah. I fired 'em plenty of times at the range. I understand why they have that front hand grip. That's a mean weapon."

"How'd you meet Cunningham and Robinson?"

"We met here. Never seen them before. They seem like decent kind."

"They're both good workers."

"They are that."

Lee Ann came into the room carrying a pitcher of lemonade and two glasses. "You men look thirsty. My lemonade has quite a reputation. A little sweet like me but also a bit tart," she smiled.

She poured a glass for each of them. "I'll be in the kitchen if you need me."

He needed her. She would be by the door listening and analyzing.

"I missed you yesterday afternoon. Where were you?"

"Huntin'. Whenever I have spare time. Didn't find nothin'. I think the deer herd out here has been thinned. Probably time we let them breed. Repopulate. I've seen lands with the herd so thin that they can't repopulate. Deer are territorial. They stick to one neighborhood."

"Where did you get your schoolin'?"

"Mostly from my mama. She was educated. Went to college. I dropped out of school at 15 and went to work. She didn't want me to, but somebody had to put food on the table. She did the best she could, but that wasn't always enough. I guess you've never seen that side of life."

"Only in Northern France. Sometimes we'd go for days with no food. Sometimes the rats in the foxholes started lookin' pretty good. I remember one time one of the men shot a big old rat. He walked around holdin' the rat by the tail and askin' who wanted to cook it. Some of the men were tempted. But you're right; I've never gone without food on a consistent basis. Cookie Custer always made plenty of money. We never wanted."

Chapter Fifty-Six

Plottin'
November 2, 1921
Harpers Ferry, West Virginia

"He's onto us. I can tell. He ain't no dummy. He brought us into that same room. I'm sure his wife was listenin'. They know what we done. You know Bos Custer. He don't take no prisoners. Either we scoot or we shoot. The shootin' has to start now if that's where we're goin'. Otherwise, we tuck tail," Crickenden said.

"Tommy's going hunting this afternoon. Why not finish the job and then report back to Capone. If we take out three of his best men, we'll get a bonus," Robinson said.

"Won't be no bonus if they kill us all in the woods. I think it's a trap. Tryin' to draw us out. They'll hang us from the nearest tree and use us for target practice. These are hard men. A lot harder than us," Crickenden said.

"What you think, Cunningham?" Robinson asked.

"I agree with both of you. Our only chance is in the woods. We attack 'em now and they gun us down like dogs. In the woods we got a chance. We got cover. We got weapons. We know they're comin' at us. I say we play along. Johnson said he was leavin' at 1:00. Get ready," Cunningham said.

The three men looked at each other. Each nodded. They knew they'd be fighting all three of the Custers that afternoon.

Chapter Fifty-Seven

Rhonda Under Suspicion
November 2, 1921
Harpers Ferry, West Virginia

"I wonder who the leak is," Bos said.

"I don't know. I like Rhonda, but she has been away for a few days over the last few weeks. I know she's just been goin' back to North Carolina to see her parents. I don't blame her for that, but some of these men happen to be from North Carolina. Is there any chance that she might have said somethin'?" Lee Ann asked.

"I don't know. She may have."

"I'll keep an eye on her. Let's not say anything to Nevin about this. We can suspect all we want, but until we have some proof, we stay mum. I feel bad even suspectin' Rhonda."

"No you don't. You're every bit as suspicious as I am about everyone. About everything. You lived in a den of vipers in Washington. Any one of them would turn on you at any moment."

"We're cut from the same cloth," Lee Ann smiled.

Chapter Fifty-Eight

The Trail
November 2, 1921
Harpers Ferry, West Virginia

Tommy Johnson was six feet tall. He weighed 180 pounds. Compact. Muscular. Focused. Determined. He carried with him a Winchester rifle. He had loaded the rifle with six rounds. Lever action. He knew how to use it. He joked that he could hit a sparrow at 200 yards. He could. His side arm was the Custer family issue of a .45. He didn't like the weapon. Too much kick. But he had learned to overcome it. He could put several rounds in a tight formation at 50 feet. In his backpack, he carried a 50-foot rope, a small crossbow that he had learned to use, and two hunting knives that were sheathed. He carried a Thompson strapped on his back. He knew the power of the Thompson, but he never cared for that weapon. It was too modern. The Winchester required skill. The Thompson required little skill.

Johnson knew he was being watched. Watched by the Capone men and also by the Custers. There were two trails. One led in a due northerly direction. The other was westerly. Each trail led to different hunting spots he knew well. Areas where deer frequented for the water. Johnson had decided he would take neither trail. He would set a new course trying to evade any of the traps that his hunters had laid. He moved between the two designated trails in a northwesterly direction. The Custers knew where he was heading. The hunters would soon know where he was heading.

By 1:00 a.m., Jasper Crickenden had set up a hunter's perch at three locations. Each was 50 feet off the ground. He chose them for hunting

The Counterattack

purposes. With that perspective, he could see a deer 300 yards away. The deer could also see, hear, and smell him. He knew that. There were ways to fool the deer. There was no way to fool Tommy Johnson. Crickenden had been in the woods most of his life. He recognized any movement. He had a hearing capacity like a wild animal. His sense of smell told him if there was a human being within 100 feet. The other men had wondered how he had developed these capabilities. His explanation was that it was from a life in the woods hunting all types of wildlife. He had to be like them. And he was.

Crickenden saw Johnson before Johnson saw him. The time difference was slight. Johnson knew that could be critical. He could see the clearing ahead in the big pine tree. He hadn't seen Crickenden. He knew the shot would only come if Crickenden had him fully sighted in.

Johnson moved from tree to tree. His footsteps were measured. His movements were from spot to spot with pauses when there was good protection.

Bos Custer and his brother, Nevin, had sighted in on Crickenden. They knew that Robinson and Cunningham were nearby. Silence was golden. This was the opportunity for Johnson to use his crossbow. Its effective range was 50 yards. They would keep an eye on Crickenden in his perch. If it looked like he had a clear shot at Johnson, then Crickenden was a dead man. It was a waiting game. Waiting for the arrow.

Crickenden exited his perch. No one saw his descent down the rope. When Johnson realized that Crickenden was not in the perch, it was too late. From 20 feet away, Cunningham's .45 barked and hit Johnson in the back of the neck. Johnson crumbled. Cunningham scrambled. Bos and Nevin knew something bad had happened. Johnson had been set up. The distraction of losing sight of Crickenden deadened Johnson's senses. He had not heard Cunningham coming up behind him. He should have. When Bos and Nevin found him, he was not breathing.

The bullet had penetrated his spine. The Custers would come back for him later. Now they were on the defensive. Everyone except Bos.

Chapter Fifty-Nine

The Trap
November 2, 1921
Harpers Ferry, West Virginia

Thomas had seen it all. As soon as Cunningham fired his .45, Thomas fired a burst from his Thompson. He was 40 yards away. Covered with leaves and branches, he had been reluctant to give up his camouflage. But he knew he may not get another clear shot at Cunningham. He had to take it. The .45 rounds hit Cunningham in the back as he was running away. Thomas took no relish in shooting a man in the back. There would be no regrets about this.

Thomas had gotten to know Cunningham. They had similar personalities. Similar likes and dislikes. Both men were single. Both men liked to talk about the women they had known. Both men liked their beer. When Thomas had learned from his brother that Cunningham may be on the payroll of Capone, he didn't believe it. He didn't want to believe it. He hadn't had that many friends. There were his brothers, but they were different. They were brothers. Cunningham had become a friend. Thomas wanted to approach the body to say goodbye to his friend. He knew that was a luxury he couldn't afford. He stayed put under the leaves and branches and hoped that no one had identified his position.

Bos and Nevin signaled to each other. They knew where Thomas was. They didn't know who else knew that. Bos had hoped that Thomas would change position. He hadn't. He knew he and Nevin had to stay close and defend Thomas's position. Capone's men would be moving in for the kill. Bos knew this could be a trap. Capone's men might sit and wait. Wait for the Custers to come for their brother. He didn't like defense. He liked offense. Bos decided to circle back and talk with Nevin. They needed a plan.

When he got close to Nevin, he whistled. Nevin heard the whistle and knew it was his older brother. A half hour later, they met and talked.

"We fell for the first trick. Let's not do that again," Bos said.

"I'll second that," Nevin said. "These guys are good. It's almost like we trained them."

"I think I might've trained some of them. I don't remember any of them. Nor do I remember the names," Bos said. "Sorry day that we train killers and then they turn around and they use those skills against us."

"So we sit tight. Our brother is the bait. Let's hope he's not too restless."

The predators did not wait long. Within an hour, Bos could see Robinson and Crickenden moving in. Robinson no doubt was the cover. Their movement was slow. When they got within 50 feet of where Thomas was hiding, both Robinson and Crickenden broke into a dash. They were moving too fast for either Nevin or Bos to get a clear shot. They must've identified how Thomas was laying because they were coming at him from behind. Thomas could hear them. Unless he sat up he could not see them. He did sit up. Robinson pointed his rifle at Thomas. Thomas fired a burst from the Thompson. He fired in a circular pattern. He hoped to increase the chances of hitting his target. One round hit Robinson in the face and stopped him. Stopped him dead. He fell back, dropped his rifle and sank to the ground.

Crickenden took cover by the nearest tree. He knew he had been spotted by all three of the Custers. He knew Cunningham was dead. He knew Robinson was down. The only way to stay alive was to retreat. Retreat he did. He ran zigzag in a southerly direction away from where the Custers were. He knew he was now outgunned. Outgunned by three gunners.

Chapter Sixty

The Trick
November 2, 1921
Harpers Ferry, West Virginia

The retreat led the Custers in a direction they were not familiar with. Crickenden knew that. He knew how aggressive the Custers were. He also respected their fighting skills. Now it was just him. One against three. He didn't mind those odds. He liked them. Cunningham had been a skillful marksman, but he didn't have the cunning and guile of Crickenden and Robinson. Both of them recognized that. Robinson had been too cocky.

Crickenden decided to head west. Capone had told them that killing Custer's three top men was the priority. Capone recognized the difficulty in killing any one of the Custers. But right now, Crickenden had the opportunity to kill all three. Crickenden liked that.

He ran a mile west. He knew this forest like the back of his hand. He knew it better than the Custers. The rock promontory presented good cover. They had dug a three-foot-deep tunnel from that promontory to another one 100 feet away. The tunnel had been covered with branches and leaves. The Custers running at full tilt might not notice it. Whether they did or not didn't matter as to the outcome.

Nevin Custer led the way. At six feet two and 170 pounds, he ran like a deer. Crickenden saw the deer coming. The deer was running too fast. Too fast to see the trench ahead. He fell in it. Crickenden heard the bone snap. Nevin fell into the trench. His whole body was now concealed. Crickenden opened fire. He had no clear shot at Nevin Custer. He knew now that their trench could not be the trick they had designed.

The Counterattack

There was no passage to the other promontory. He recognized that he needed to stay on the move and keep the Custers in sight. Bos Custer would come to the aid of his fallen brother. That was Crickenden's target.

Thomas had a clear shot at Crickenden. He took it with his Winchester. The trigger pull was easy. The round hit Crickenden in the left shoulder. Thomas moved the lever quickly. Chambered another round and fired. Crickenden moved to his left. He knew he had to. He knew there would be a second round in quick succession. It missed. Crickenden stood behind the nearby tree and brought the Winchester to his right shoulder. He had to balance it on a small limb on the tree. His left shoulder was useless, bleeding and burning. He fired off the first round. He didn't know which of the Custers was his target. He figured it probably was not Bos. There seldom were misses with Bos. He brought the Winchester back to his side and put the muzzle on the ground to move the lever. As he did so, the round pierced the upper part of his right ear. Crickenden winced.

Thomas knew he had hit his target. Thomas stayed protected. He didn't know where Bos was. He knew where Nevin was. He figured Bos was nearby. To Crickenden's left, Thomas saw movement. Of all the shooters, Robinson was the most skilled. And the most feared. Crickenden was close second. The first round was just a warning. Crickenden hit Thomas's Winchester at the firing mechanism. The round altered the trigger. It was useless. Thomas threw it down. He carried a Thompson over his shoulder. He had never cared much for the Thompson, especially in a wooded area. Thomas moved closer to the rock promontory. He knew the other shooter would be coming at him. He might as well meet him head-on.

Chapter Sixty-One

The Triumph
November 2, 1921
Harpers Ferry, West Virginia

Bos saw Nevin in the trench. He figured it connected the two promontories. He ran toward the promontory that was most northerly. He saw the disturbed ground. He entered the trench low-crawling inches at a time. Fifty feet ahead he saw Nevin. It was unclear whether he was conscious. As he approached, he reached out his hand to Nevin and whispered, "Brother, you still with me?" Nevin didn't respond. He did squeeze Bos's hand. Bos pulled Nevin toward him. It was going to be a slow movement back to the promontory from which he came. The firing resumed. Crickenden figured Bos was in the trench. He couldn't see any human form. He heard movement. He knew gunfire must be effective. What he didn't know was that Thomas had a Thompson submachine gun. He soon heard it.

Thomas had brought six circular drums of ammunition. He opened up with continuous fire at the location where he sensed Crickenden was holed up. He planned to keep him pinned down. At least this way Crickenden couldn't be taking shots at Bos or Nevin.

What Thomas had not experienced is what one man with a Winchester could do. Crickenden flipped his rifle back-and-forth using only one arm. One round at the tunnel. One round in the direction of Thomas. He knew how to fire. Fire with accuracy. Rechamber quickly and fire again. He wasn't putting out as much lead as Thomas. His shots were effective.

The Counterattack

Bos dragged Nevin behind the rock promontory. He said to himself that the compound fracture needed to be treated quickly. He took off his shirt and applied it to Nevin's right leg above the knee. The tourniquet would have to suffice for the moment. "I'm going to help Thomas. I'll be back as soon as I can."

Nevin nodded.

Bos decided to take the high ground. He ran from tree to tree to the other rock promontory. There he scampered up the rocks to the highest point. He fired a round 20 feet over Thomas's head. He wanted Thomas to hold fire. Bos didn't see Crickenden, but he did hear him. He heard the lever action. He heard the heavy breathing.

Bos had retrieved from Tommy Johnson's backpack fifty feet of rope. He tied it into a lasso. Bos stood up and rotated the rope overhead. He threw it to where he believed Crickenden was standing. It worked. He could feel it cinch around Crickenden's body. Bos began running with it. Crickenden followed but lost his footing. Now he was being dragged by Boston Custer. There was no stopping Custer. He dragged him until it was clear there was no breath left in Crickenden. He ran back to where Crickenden lay, pulled out his .45, and shot him in the head.

Chapter Sixty-Two

The Pickup
November 2, 1921
Harpers Ferry, West Virginia

The bone poked through the quad area. Bos knew he needed immediate attention. Nevin was chomping on a piece of cloth. Bos couldn't imagine the pain level. They both had seen worse in Northern France. Sometimes men walking around with no arms. Sometimes hobbling with one leg. A missing limb torn from its socket. Scenes that all three of the Custers never forgot. Bos would never forget this one. It was his brother. It was personal. It would be avenged.

Bos looked at Thomas and said, "You stay here with Nevin. I'll run up to the house and make a portable cot. That way we can carry him, and when we put him down, he'll be on a cot as opposed to the ground. I should be back in 30 minutes."

Bos looked at Nevin and said, "Don't you go anywhere."

The return smile was there. But faint.

Bos began his run. It was almost three miles back to the house. He made it in less than twenty minutes. He sent one of the men into Harpers Ferry to get a doctor. He didn't know how much time it would take to get Nevin back to the house. Plus, he didn't want the tourniquet staying on too long. Whether a doctor would be able to reset this fracture was something Bos was unfamiliar with. It was a mean fracture. The thigh bone must've actually collapsed when Nevin hit the trench.

"I assume it didn't go well. What happened?" a female voice said.

Bos looked around and saw Lee Ann.

The Counterattack

"Nevin is hurt. He fell in a trench and broke his thigh bone. It's serious. Why don't you head down there and see if you can help out. I'll be down in a few minutes once I make a stretcher that can serve as a cot."

"I'll get my pants on. I can ride down there. Where exactly is he?"

Bos gave her the directions. "You're probably gonna hear him cryin' out. He's in a lot of pain."

Bos set to work. The two-by-fours served as the main elements. He wrapped the canvas around the two-by-fours and secured the canvas with small nails. He cut out handholds on each end of the two-by-fours. Bos cut two shorter pieces of two-by-fours. He fixed them at the center with a screw. The cross-bracing was with one-by-fours. It stabilized the bracing to allow the stretcher to be supported for use as a cot. Within twenty minutes he was finished. He ran back to where his brother was with his handiwork on his shoulder.

When he arrived back, he could hear Nevin groaning as he approached. Lee Ann was on her knees bent over him. She had managed to realign the two separated pieces of the thigh bone. The break in the bones had been a clean one. The ends needed to be rejoined and stabilized so they could grow back together. She was in the process of putting a brace on Nevin's thigh to stabilize her handiwork.

"Is there anything you can't do?" Bos asked.

"No time for that now. Find me a better limb that is straighter than this one. We need to keep this leg straight."

Bos looked around for another limb that fit the description. He saw one 20 feet away. He ran for it and brought it back to his wife. She applied it to the inside of Nevin's thigh and then wrapped the leg with part of the dress she had brought with her so that the juxtaposed tree limbs kept the thigh straight.

"He's ready. Let's get him on the stretcher and get him home," Lee Ann ordered. Bos and Thomas complied.

The trek back to the house was slow. They knew they couldn't run while carrying Nevin. By the time they arrived, the doctor from town was there. He had heard about the Custers' complex, but never seen it. He had no idea that the owners were Black. His medical practice treated all. A number of freed slaves had settled in Harpers Ferry. His waiting room in his office was always filled with people of different colors. He looked at Nevin's leg and asked, "Who did this?"

No one answered.

"Well, I guess he did it himself," the doctor said.

"My wife did it," Bos said.

The doctor was getting an eyeful today. He looked at Lee Ann. He looked at Bos. He looked back at Nevin. He asked Lee Ann, "Would you like to come work for me and be my nurse?"

"I have a full-time job," she smiled.

"This was nicely set. Nice and straight. I couldn't have done any better myself. You've also controlled the bleeding. Well done. Why did you call me?"

"I've set fractures like this before. But this one seemed worse than the others. I just needed your reassurance. He is my brother-in-law after all."

"Family can be demanding," the doctor smiled. "You just need to keep the wound clean. I brought some splints with me, which I'll apply. I think we've done everything we can do. I'll take a look in a few days to make sure everything is fusing nice and straight. Good work, young lady."

"Now all I need is someone to put some full-body splints on my husband so he doesn't go off and do something stupid," Lee Ann said.

The doctor didn't know what to make of that.

Chapter Sixty-Three

Plannin'
November 3, 1921
Harpers Ferry, West Virginia

The pain level abated. Not by much. Nevin was sitting up. He was eating. He carried on conversations without wanting to curl up in pain. He felt he might even mend.

"I don't know what you would've done if you caught Crickenden. Crickenden had a good laugh. Of course we had the last laugh, since we're still here. He's not. The three bodies are down by the bunkhouse. Bos went into DC last night. He's looking for recruits. He says we need 10 more men. That's just to make up for your loss," Thomas laughed.

"Your kind words are reassurin', brother. Even if they are not true. What I need to know is when can I get up and start movin'?"

"Right now," came a female voice. Nevin looked to his left and saw Lee Ann coming at him with crutches.

"They're a little bit too long for me. We measured you last night when you were sleepin'. Good thing you're forced to sleep on your back with a broken leg. I think we got an accurate measurement. Now is the time to find out," Lee Ann said.

Thomas and Lee Ann helped Nevin stand up on his good leg. They put a crutch under each arm and stood back. The look in his eyes was one of terror. Sheer terror. This man who had fought through Northern France was terrified of being on crutches. He could not run. He could not shoot. He would have to learn how to defend himself. He would be dependent on his wife, Rhonda.

He was so ashamed of his injury that he didn't want his wife to see him. She had spent the night by his side while he slept. He stirred and cried out all night. She tried to comfort him. He had no awareness she was even there. When the sun rose, she left his side so that he would think his command to his wife was being followed. It was not. She was looking over him from a distance.

She was in the next room. Listening. And crying. This strong man needed her. She was determined to be there.

She walked into the room. "Stop your bellyaching. Let me see you use those crutches and come over here. I need a hug and a kiss," Rhonda said.

He moved the two crutches forward by an inch. His body swung forward an equal amount. The next movement was two inches. "You're getting the hang of it," Rhonda said. "Try taking a big boy step."

Nevin shook his head. He couldn't believe he was surrounded by his family. He felt humiliated. He felt loved. He felt like he better follow his wife's command. He took a big boy step. Rhonda applauded. "I knew you had it in you. I knew the big boy was somewhere. I think we found him. Two more steps and you're home."

"What are you all lookin' at? I remember Bos gave you instructions to start plannin' the attack on Capone. It doesn't look to me like you're doin' much plannin'. Bos don't want to hear that you taught me how to use crutches. He probably expects me to be walkin' already."

Chapter Sixty-Four

Recruitin'
November 3, 1921
Washington, DC

The Custer house at 520 T Street, N.W., looked the same. It had been closed up for several months. When Bos entered, he could smell the dust. It was everywhere. He left the front door open and walked to the back of the house and opened that door. November in DC could be very pleasant. This day was. The sun was out. There was a breeze. It ruffled the curtains in the front of the house when he opened the windows. Perfect day for letting the house air out. It needed it. It needed a lot of attention. He thought there were a whole lot of things that needed attention. His family needed attention. Once he finished with Capone, his family would be his only priority.

Bos figured the house might be habitable by the time he returned that evening. When he got back, he would start cleaning. At least the musty air should have cleared.

He recalled where Alvin Morrison had lived. He figured that was as good a place as any to start. He knocked on the front door. The last time he'd been here, Alvin had been upstairs with one of his lady friends. Alvin had not been too happy that Bos was interrupting.

He missed Alvin. The two men were much alike. Loners. Independent. Set their own course. And followed it. No one answered the knocks at the front door. Bos went around back. He approached the rear door stoop. The door opened and two Black man came running out. They were as surprised as Bos was. Neither expected to see the other. Bos tackled the first man and drove him into the second man. Both men were on the ground. Bos jumped up quickly and unholstered his .45.

"Who the hell are you?" Bos asked.

"Who the hell are you?" the first man said.

"I'm a friend of Alvin Morrison's," Bos replied.

"I am his brother," the first man said.

"Bos Custer. You probably heard of me."

"You bet I have. Alvin talked about you. He talked about your boats. Sometimes I worked on the boat with Alvin. We never met before. My name is Josh. I'm Alvin's younger brother. This is my friend Washington. We call him 'Wash'".

Bos holstered his sidearm. "How come you ran away?"

"We thought you were from the bank. Bank ain't getting paid. They say they're going to take the house. Alvin always had the money to pay. Paid on time."

"I can help with that. But I need somethin'. I need 10 men. Men who know weapons and know how to fight. I'll pay 'em. I'll pay 'em well. The work is dangerous."

"We might be able to do business. There are a whole lot of veterans here who can't find work. Good men. But they're getting into trouble. You give them some work to do, and they'll do it. Why don't you come with me over to 10th Street. There's an empty lot there. That's where they gather about this time of day."

Bos helped the man off the ground. They shook hands.

"I like what I'm hearin'," Bos said.

Chapter Sixty-Five

Suspicions Allayed
November 7, 1921
Harpers Ferry, West Virginia

"Suspicions allayed?" Bos asked.

"Suspicions allayed," Lee Ann responded.

"Capone planned well. Rhonda had nothin' to do with these three killers. They were recruited and paid by Capone."

"We should both feel bad about ever suspectin' Rhonda."

"Now you're makin' me feel bad. Who suspected Rhonda first? You or me?"

"I suspect it was simultaneous. We seem to think alike."

"That's scary, isn't it?"

"You might say that. I think it's romantic." She moved toward him.

Chapter Sixty-Six

The Gauntlet
November 7, 1921
Harpers Ferry, West Virginia

The 10 new men were battle hardened. They had fought on the streets of Washington. They had fought in the fields of Northern France. Bos liked what he saw. Tough men who would kill anything that moved. Show no mercy. Expect no mercy.

"I paid you all upfront. I paid you well. Every man got the same. The same $500. There'll be another thousand dollars for you if you return. If you don't return, you need to put in writin' where you want your thousand dollars to go. I will personally make sure the money is delivered. What I'm askin' of you is a lot. We're goin' to Chicago. We're goin' there to kill some very tough men. Very tough men who killed some friends of mine. Killed them here at this settlement. They would've killed me and my brothers. But they couldn't. They will try to kill you. They will show you no mercy. I expect you to show no mercy. We have two days to get ready, and then we leave. In those two days, I'm gonna test your battle skills. We'll find out what you're made of. Do any of you have any questions?" Bos asked the 10 men.

Bos had already decided that his battle group would consist of these 10 men, his brother Thomas, and a total of four other men from the two mining communities whom he had helped out. Nevin was immobile.

Bos wanted to make sure these men could follow orders, stay in formation when that was necessary, and kill whether it was necessary or not. He had sent word to the two mining communities that he needed two volunteers from each. He wanted fighters. He wanted killers. There

The Counterattack

were plenty within those two groups. He expected them to arrive later today.

"We're gonna start with a three-mile run. Anyone who can't do that?"

No one responded.

"Each of you has a pack. The pack is loaded with all the supplies you will need. Each pack weighs about 30 pounds. Some of you have Springfields. Some have Mausers. I prefer the Mausers, but we only had so many. You know the drill."

The men picked up their packs. They slung them over the right shoulders and looped their left arms through the other strap. They picked up their rifles and brought them to port arms. In single file, they stepped off. First a slow trot. Then Bos picked up the pace.

Bos was impressed. These men had been home from the war for more than two years. They had kept themselves in shape. A three-mile run tired all of them, but they were ready to keep going.

"Do any of you know explosives?" Bos asked.

Two men raised their hands.

"You with the beard, what's your experience with explosives?"

"I blew up more than 20 bridges in Northern France. They were bridges that the Germans had hoped to use. I disabled them," the bearded man said.

"How about you?" Bos asked the other man.

"Same. We worked together. We're a team. You get one, you get the other. No splitting us up."

"I like that. A team. Just don't forget you're part of a bigger team. We'll talk about explosives at the end of the day," Bos said.

Lee Ann and Rhonda had made lunch for all 12 of them. They sat down together and ate. The nearby stream was the source of water. It was the same stream that fed the stills. Bos knew the water was good. The men knew it was cold.

After lunch, Bos and Thomas fixed targets at 100 yards. Bos wanted to see if the men could shoot. He set up a single firing line. Ten targets. Each target was a large pumpkin. Lee Ann had brought them down from the pumpkin patch. They were each at least two feet in diameter. Each weighed at least 10 pounds.

Nine of the men hit the target with their first shot. One man who missed the first two shots hit the target with his third shot.

"There's no room for error here," Bos said to the man who had missed. "No room at all. Let's try it again."

This time, Bos set up a single target at 150 yards. The man was asked to get back into a prone position and commence firing. He knew his continued employment depended on hitting his target. He did.

"Good shootin'. That's what I need to see every time. I don't think we're gonna need any shootin' at 100 yards. But you never know. Battles are unpredictable."

Bos liked this group. They didn't say much. They followed orders. They were in good shape, and they knew how to shoot. He had seen what he wanted to see. Ten men who would follow orders and kill everything that moved.

Chapter Sixty-Seven

Guinevere
November 9, 1921
Chicago, Illinois

Lee Ann's trip west was uneventful. Thomas went with her. His carrying case had no clothes in it. It was loaded with ammunition and his Thompson. He hoped he would not need anything in the case.

Lee Ann had been overseeing the brothels for over a year. They were money-makers. She had two women who lived in Chicago who managed the multiple houses. They treated the women fairly and paid them well. Lee Ann figured someone was going to make this money. It might as well be her and her husband.

She gathered her two lieutenants. "We're gonna need all 15 of the houses. Give the girls a week off with full pay. Not just full pay but pay and a half. Pay them all 50 percent more than what they would make in a week. But they need to clear out. Best they leave town. Tell them to think of it as a well-deserved vacation. The men who will be comin' to these houses startin' tomorrow are not men who any of these women want to meet."

One of the women asked what was going on.

"The less you know the better," Lee Ann said.

The man who entered did not knock. He was a tall man. One hundred eighty pounds. Black hair and a black mustache. Pale complected. He looked like Black Irish. The fact that his name ended in a vowel told her he was not Irish. Lee Ann withdrew the .32 pistol from her purse. She kept it in her lap under the table. He was clueless that she was armed.

"I need to know what's going on, Guinevere. You ain't been here in months. Something's going on." He opened up his double-breasted coat to expose a revolver on his left hip. Cross-draw. He probably thought it looked good. It might but it slowed down the ability to unholster the weapon.

Lee Ann was wondering where Thomas was. He must've seen the man enter. Lee Ann had to assume she was on her own.

"We were just talkin' about a ladies' charity. We're tryin' to promote women's suffrage. The movement needs money. Would you like to contribute?" Lee Ann smiled.

"Look, lady, ain't got time for your smart talk. Tell me what you were talking about, or this one here will get smacked," the man said, referring to one of Lee Ann's lieutenants.

Lee Ann stood up and pointed the .32 pistol at the man's head. "You won't be smackin' anyone if I put a bullet in your head. I want you to run back to Mr. Capone and tell him that we've reorganized the houses. His income is up. But we control the houses. We'll do as we please. Do you understand?"

"I sure do. But Mr. Capone ain't gonna like this."

"I don't much care what Mr. Capone likes. But tell him Guinevere was here."

She escorted him to the door and down the stairway. She saw him hop into a four-door sedan that was parked in front of the house.

Lee Ann smiled. Guinevere? *Since when did I take on that role*, she asked herself and smiled.

Just then Thomas walked in. "I know what you're thinkin'. I saw him enter. I gave him a couple of minutes. I knew you had your .32. I know you can shoot. You weren't left alone. I know better."

Chapter Sixty-Eight

The Round Table
November 10, 1921
Chicago, Illinois

Mike Burke knew Chicago. His father ran the numbers racket throughout the city. He had attempted to compete with Capone with speakeasies and liquor. That did not go well. Burke was squeezed out. Capone could have snuffed him out, but Burke was smart enough to realize he was no match for Capone. They both backed off. They both survived.

Burke always kept his ear to the ground. He knew what was going on in Capone's camp. He knew Capone couldn't keep up with the demand for alcohol. Capone's customers were from all corners. All deals were cash tendered at the time of delivery. Burke had heard that Capone was planning a sit down of all of his bosses and chiefs. Unlike Johnny Torrio, Capone didn't tolerate disobedience. Everyone knew his rules. They were simple. All cash is delivered to the central Capone repository. There is no skimming. Capone organized his chiefs and bosses below them in a hierarchy. At the top were three chiefs. Below them were the bosses. The chiefs divided Chicago, Detroit, Ohio, Indiana, and New York City among them. Seventy percent of the booze in the US was consumed in those areas. Capone controlled all of the traffic in those areas. His three chiefs had told him of instances of skimming. All of the bosses and chiefs were being summoned to Chicago for a lesson. Burke figured that some of the bosses would not be going home.

"Any information you can give me about this would be appreciated, Burke. I know you don't owe me anything. But we do have a common enemy," Bos said over the phone.

"Capone is big on symbols. The meeting is November 11 at 11:11 a.m. The date and time the armistice was signed. The other knuckleheads won't understand what Capone is doing. They may think he's calling this meeting to ask for concessions or to surrender some of his power. Capone's idea is just the opposite. He'll come into this meeting with a baseball bat or a Thompson. Some of his bosses may feel these weapons. The speaking end of the weapons," Burke said.

"Is there any way you can get me the location?"

"I'm working on that. I've got a guy inside who should know tonight where the meet is taking place. You'll know when I know."

"Thanks, Burke." Bos knew he didn't deserve a friend as loyal as Burke.

Bos had a strange way of generating loyalty. The men who were loyal to him were uncertain if that loyalty was based on admiration or based on fear. Bos generated both emotions. Both in people close to him and people who knew him from a distance.

Bos smiled. Maybe there would be retribution for Tommy Johnson, Jack Jackson, and Hiram Walker. Just maybe.

Chapter Sixty-Nine

Excalibur
November 11, 1921
Chicago, Illinois

The location was unexpected. Capone's focus of operation had moved outside of the city. The warehouse where the meeting was taking place was in the center of the Levee. Bos thought Lee Ann had returned to Harpers Ferry. She hadn't. She was waiting in a car with Thomas at 10:30 a.m. when Bos arrived.

He was not happy.

"You didn't think I was gonna let you do this alone did you?" Lee Ann asked.

"I didn't think anything. I told you to come out here and get back home," Bos said. "You're too valuable to lose. I can't afford to lose you."

"I can't afford to lose you. You're too valuable to lose," she smiled.

"I guess we're in this together. I know you can use that." Bos looked at the Thompson Lee Ann was holding. "I'm not lookin' for a bloodbath. Capone has three chiefs. They run everything from Chicago eastward. Those are the three I want. Keep your Thompson on single shot unless things get crazy. You'll know who the good guys are by the color of their skin," he smiled.

She had come prepared. She wore a soft sole shoe and pants. She had on work gloves that fit tightly on her fingers. She was ready. Ready for anything.

The warehouse had a 30-foot ceiling. The roof was supported by steel I-beams that rested on concrete vertical pillars. Whoever had built the warehouse was sensitive to the heavy snows in Chicago. The roof was not flat. It was a slight A-frame.

All 10 of Bos's men were on the roof. They had been there since 7:00 a.m. Bos and Lee Ann climbed up to the area at the bottom of the gable on the east side of the warehouse. There was a point of entry there.

The cars began pulling up shortly before 11:00 a.m. Each of them carried two bodyguards and one boss. They filed into the warehouse and assumed their assigned seats. Each seat had a nameplate. Capone was the last to enter. He sat at the side of the round table that was closest to the exit. At 11:11 a.m., he called the meeting to order.

As he began speaking, three Thompson machine guns from Bos's men above began to speak. One Thompson hit the center of the table. It stitched a circle in the center of the table, which collapsed inward. The two other Thompsons sprayed a steady stream of bullets around the perimeter of the men at the table. Everybody stayed in their position.

Bos and LeeAnn rappelled down from the gable on the far end of the building. They strolled toward the table. Capone put his hands on his hips.

"Show me who your three chiefs are, Capone. Now. Or I put a bullet in your head," Bos demanded.

"It's the three of us," one of the men said pointing to two others.

Without any hesitation Bos shot all three men in the head.

"You were supposed to leave one of them for me. I told Tommy I would do that for him," Lee Ann said.

"I know. We can draw lots over Capone. No. I take that back. Capone, you walk away today. I like the way you control things. I hope you know I can hit you anytime I want. You stay on your side of the street, and I'll stay on mine. I like dealing with the devil I know. I don't want to deal with the devil I don't know. That's all we got to understand."

Bos took his wife's hand and walked out of the building.

About the Author

Brien A. Roche: After four years as a patrol officer with the Washington D.C. Metropolitan Police Department and 45 years as a trial lawyer in the Washington, D.C. area, I have "been around the barn."

Since being admitted to the practice of law in Virginia in 1976, I have tried more than 300 jury cases to conclusion and handled thousands of other cases of every conceivable type. In 1985, I became a partner with the firm of Johnson & Roche in McLean, Virginia. My practice has been principally litigation with a focus on tort litigation along with substantial involvement in commercial litigation, real estate litigation and domestic relations litigation.

My interest in writing fiction ties in with my interest in the study of history. The main character in the *Prohibition* series is not a historical character but he acts as part of some historical events including the race riot of July 19, 1919 in Washington, D.C. Most of the other events are purely fictional but many of the characters of course are not. The existence of the Liberator boats is fact-based as these water crafts were constructed as part of the U.S. war effort in Europe. The integration of fact and fiction is always tricky but hopefully these novels instill some further interest in the reader in this historical era and in further historical exploration. Visit www.brienrocheauthor.com

Now Available!

BRIEN A. ROCHE'S

THE PROHIBITION SERIES
BOOK ONE – BOOK 2

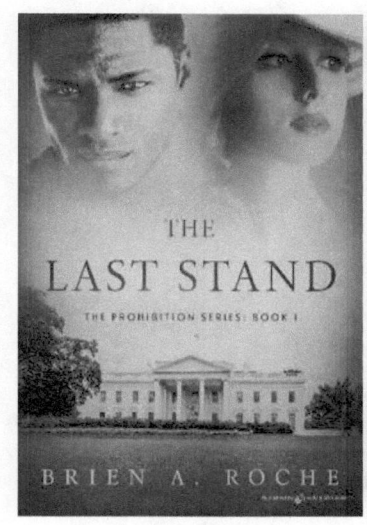 

For more information
visit: www.SpeakingVolumes.us

Now Available!

DICK BROWN'S

UNDER THE CANYON SKY SERIES
BOOKS 1 - 3

 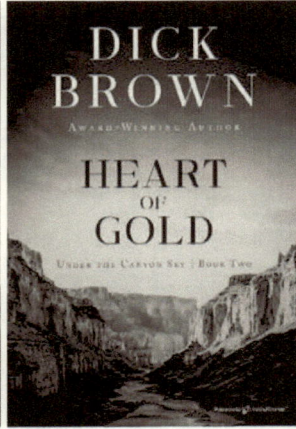 

**For more information
visit: www.SpeakingVolumes.us**

Now Available!

R.G. YOHO'S
ACTION / ADVENTURE WESTERNS

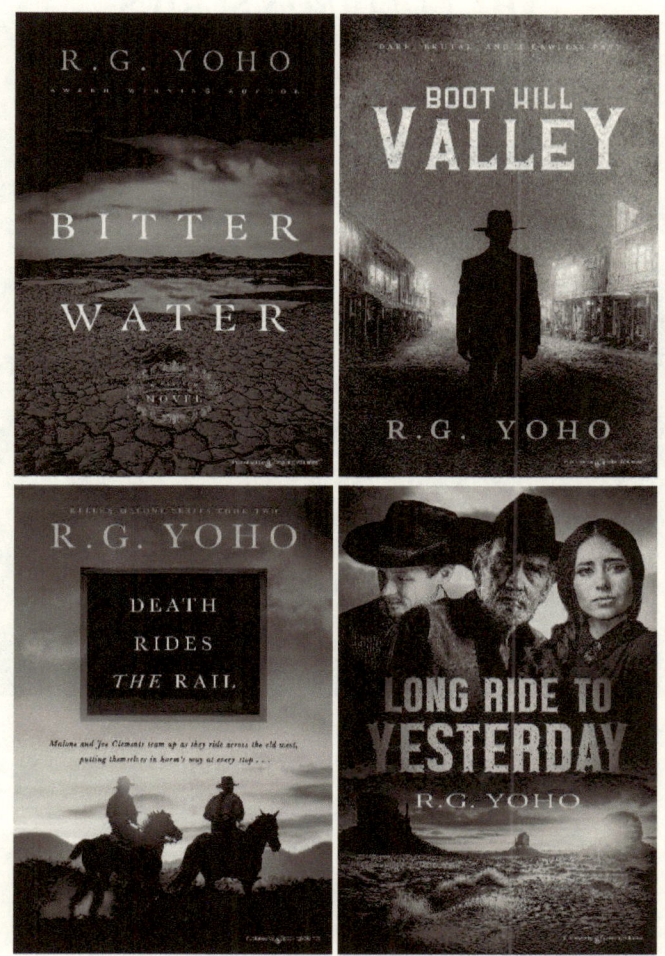

For more information
visit: www.SpeakingVolumes.us

Now Available!

F.M. PARKER'S

BEST-SELLING AUTHOR OF THE *COLDIRON* SERIES

HISTORICAL NOVELS

**For more information
visit: www.SpeakingVolumes.us**

www.ingramcontent.com/pod-product-compliance
Lightning Source LLC
LaVergne TN
LVHW041712070526
838199LV00045B/1305